"I Can't Leave You Alone, Ginny Lea,"

he murmured roughly, and pulled her forward so she slid off the chair and onto her knees on the floor.

Before she could protest, his mouth covered hers in a hard, punishing kiss. Her lips parted in a gasp, admitting his seeking, plundering tongue. She struggled, pounding her fists on his back, but his arms tightened around her waist.

The kiss was so intense that she was totally unprepared when he suddenly unclasped her arms from around him and pushed her away. His breath was coming in short rasping pants as he stood and looked down at her bewildered, upturned face.

"Oh, no, Ginny Lea," he said. "I can't leave you alone, because you belong to me. I never filed those annulment papers. Like it or not, you're still my wife!"

PHYLLIS HALLDORSON,
like all her heroines, is as in love with her husband today as on the day they met. It is because she has known so much love in her own life that her characters seem to come alive as they, too, discover the joys of romance.

Dear Reader:

I'd like to take this opportunity to thank you for all your support and encouragement of Silhouette Romances.

Many of you write in regularly, telling us what you like best about Silhouette, which authors are your favorites. This is a tremendous help to us as we strive to publish the best contemporary romances possible.

All the romances from Silhouette Books are for you, so enjoy this book and the many stories to come.

Karen Solem
Editor-in-Chief
Silhouette Books

PHYLLIS HALLDORSON
If Ever I Loved You

Silhouette *Romance*

Published by Silhouette Books New York

America's Publisher of Contemporary Romance

Silhouette Books by Phyllis Halldorson

Temporary Bride (ROM #31)
To Start Again (ROM #79)
Mountain Melody (ROM #247)
If Ever I Loved You (ROM #282)

SILHOUETTE BOOKS, a Division of Simon & Schuster, Inc.
1230 Avenue of the Americas, New York, N.Y. 10020

Copyright © 1984 by Phyllis Halldorson

Distributed by Pocket Books

ISBN: 0-671-57282-2

First Silhouette Books printing March, 1984

10 9 8 7 6 5 4 3 2 1

Map by Ray Lundgren

SILHOUETTE, SILHOUETTE ROMANCE and colophon are
registered trademarks of Simon & Schuster, Inc.
America's Publisher of Contemporary Romance

Printed in the U.S.A.

For Ethel Bangert, my teacher, who opened the door and pointed the way. With many thanks.

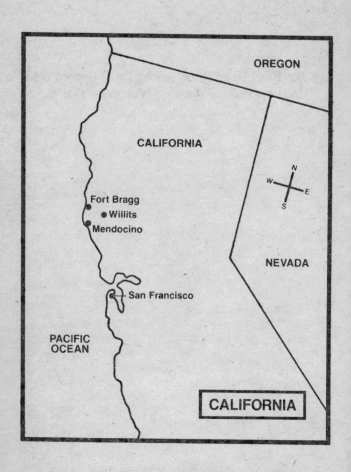

Chapter One

The somber feeling of dread intensified, tying Gina's stomach in knots. She shifted uneasily on the highly polished oak pew in the beautiful old Episcopal cathedral as the magnificent pipe organ began the processional.

A blonde girl, wraithlike in pastel pink, stepped through the door at the back of the candlelit nave and began her slow trek up the long, white-satin-covered aisle toward the altar. She was followed at suitable intervals by five other young women gowned in muted shades of yellow, blue, green, apricot and mauve. After the appearance of the maid of honor the music switched to the happy strains of Wagner's Wedding March and Cynthia, radiantly lovely in white peau de soie and lace, appeared on the arm of her father, Stewart Tobias.

Gina's nails dug into her palms as she rose with the several hundred other guests and turned to watch the glowing young bride and the handsome bearded man, who looked every inch the successful writer in his gray

7

tuxedo. For the past seven years Gina had used any excuse, truthful or not, to avoid attending weddings, but this time there had been no escape. Stewart, the strong, gentle man whose engagement diamond she wore, would never have understood her refusal to attend the marriage of his only daughter. He didn't know that seven years ago, at the age of eighteen, Gina had also walked down the flower-strewn aisle of a fashionable church here in San Francisco on the arm of her father.

Her vision blurred and in her mind it was no longer Stewart and Cynthia standing there but her father and herself, Joseph and Virginia Lea Brown. Her gown had been a dreamlike confection whipped up by one of the country's top designers, paid for, as were all the other expenses of the wedding, by her soon-to-be in-laws. Joe had looked self-conscious and uncomfortable in the first tuxedo he'd ever worn.

She'd been known as Ginny Lea in those days, a happy carefree teenager just starting her freshman year at San Francisco State University, and she had the world by the tail. It didn't matter that she was the daughter of a midwestern farm boy who had found a career in the army as a non-commissioned officer, and the man waiting for her at the altar, Peter Van Housen, was the youngest son of one of the most wealthy and prestigious families in the bay area. She was Cinderella and Peter was Prince Charming and fairy tales always ended happily.

A ragged sigh escaped before Gina could stop it, and she blinked her wide violet eyes with surprise to find that the music had stopped and Cynthia and Stewart were now standing at the altar. The white-robed clergyman asked, "Who gives Cynthia in marriage?" and Stewart answered, "Her mother and I do," then took his place in the front pew beside his ex-wife. He and Cindy's mother had had an amiable divorce and had done a remarkable job of keeping any bitterness they may have felt toward each other out of their relationship with their only child.

A wave of pain washed over Gina as she thought of her own annulment and the agony that surrounded it, and she clutched the back of the pew ahead of her to steady herself. Oh, why had she been fool enough to come today? Why hadn't she done something, anything, broken a leg if necessary, to convince Stewart that she couldn't attend?

She felt a firm, soft hand cover hers and looked up to see Twyla Sisson standing next to her, a look of concern on her round pretty face. "Gina, are you all right?" she whispered. "You're white as a ghost."

Gina wasn't the least sure she was all right, but she managed a weak smile for Twyla, her teacher, employer, confidante, and friend, and whispered back, "I'm okay, just a little too warm. It's awfully stuffy in here."

Twyla didn't look convinced but said nothing more as the guests resumed their seats and the bridal couple began taking their vows.

Gina heard the vows from her own wedding. "Do you, Virginia, take this man, Peter—?"

Oh yes, she most definitely had taken Peter Van Housen to be her lawfully wedded husband. "To have and to hold—." But of course that was what it had all been about, to have and to hold. Their physical desire for each other had been all-consuming, but Gina's strong midwestern bible belt upbringing had taught her that it was a sin to have sex before marriage. It had taken all her strength to resist Peter's pleas to go to bed with him, but finally he couldn't stand the frustration any longer and had asked her to marry him. They'd known each other less than six weeks when, over the objections of both sets of parents, they'd repeated their wedding vows in front of a handful of her friends and a church-full of San Francisco's wealthiest, most socially prominent citizens. All strangers to her.

Four hours later her marriage and her world lay shattered at her feet.

Abruptly a burst of organ music startled Gina out of her reverie and she was appalled to discover that tears had welled in her eyes and spilled down her cheeks. Cindy and her Bob, their faces glowing with excitement, were coming back up the aisle as Gina fumbled blindly in her purse for a handkerchief.

Beside her Twyla spoke in a voice tinged with alarm. "Gina, honey, for heaven's sake what's the matter? Do you feel faint?" She put her hand on Gina's arm. "Come on, let me help you out of here."

Gina found her handkerchief and dabbed at her swimming eyes. "No, please Twyla, I don't want to cause a scene. Just sit quietly and we'll leave when our turn comes."

Outside Gina breathed in the cool, moist ocean air and blinked the last of the tears from her pain-filled eyes. Tears, for heaven's sake! After seven years she could still shed tears over Peter Van Housen! What an idiot she was. He wasn't worth one tear and she'd shed buckets of them in the months following that disastrous day, but she'd finally cried herself dry and vowed that no man would ever hurt her that way again.

It hadn't been hard to keep men at a distance. She'd poured all the love and passion she had to give into her relationship with Peter and he had trampled it in the dust. There was none left, and for that she was grateful. For five years after the annulment she had dated only occasionally and she'd never gone out with the same man more than twice. It was no sacrifice, after a golden god like Peter Van Housen all other men were colorless and unexciting.

In spite of her resolve not to let it, an image of Peter formed in her mind's eye. Tall, slender, with hair the color of moonbeams and eyes the blue of the sea. His shoulders were broad, his hips slim, and his thighs firm and muscular as revealed by the tight jeans and slacks he wore.

The hair on his chest was surprisingly dark and she'd teased him about it as she'd slowly wound her fingers through it, giggling when she'd felt his heart-beat speed up. He'd called her a tease and had kissed her with a thoroughness that had left her gasping. She'd almost given herself to him that time. Would her life have been different if she had?

Once more Twyla spoke her name and Gina shook her head to dislodge the unwanted thoughts. "Do you want to stop in the rest room before we go on to the hotel for the reception?" asked Twyla. "You don't look at all well."

Gina smiled at her concerned friend. "I'm not going to be sick if that's what you're afraid of, but I do need to repair my make-up. Have you any idea where we can find a mirror?"

The mirror in the cramped little rest room wasn't very well lighted, but Gina could see all she needed to. Her creamy flawless skin required little make-up and her black mascara and mauve eye shadow were waterproof so the tears had done little damage. She applied a light film of powder and some blusher to camouflage the whiteness of her face and ran a brush through her short raven curls.

Twyla tugged at the panty girdle she wore to keep her ample curves in line and sighed disgustedly. "If I gain one more pound I'm going to have to buy all new clothes. You know something, Gina Brown? If you weren't my very dearest friend I'd hate you. You can eat anything and never grow out of a size seven."

Gina grinned. Twyla was a striking woman, queen-sized but beautifully proportioned with thick auburn hair that she usually wore in a twist up the back of her head, and warm brown eyes with golden highlights. At thirty-nine she was an unlikely cross between earth mother and femme fatale with one broken marriage and several casual love affairs in her past, a lucrative career as gallery owner and artist in her present, and who knows what in her future. She was fourteen years older than Gina, but their seven-year friendship had filled an aching void in both their lives.

"You're gorgeous and you know it," teased Gina. "Really, that gown was an inspired choice. The turquoise does exciting things to your coloring, and the long skirt drapes so gracefully around your ankles." She sighed as she put the small brush back in her evening purse. "I'd give anything for a little of your height."

Twyla eyed Gina and snorted. "Anyone who's built like you doesn't need a thing from the likes of me. It's you small gals that the men flock around, you make them feel protective. And speaking of dresses, yours is a stunner. Wish I could wear that flamingo color, but with my hair I'd look like a sunset in flight."

She picked up her hand-knit stole and headed for

the door. "We'd better get going, the reception is due to start at eight and the hotel is clear across town."

Gina settled her white angora jacket around her shoulders and followed Twyla. Ah yes, there was still the reception to get through, and that may prove to be the hardest part of all. She shuddered slightly and wondered how long it would be before she could slip quietly upstairs to the room Stewart had reserved for Twyla and her. The room where she could escape to lick her wounds in private.

The reception line was almost finished by the time Twyla and Gina arrived at the luxurious high-rise hotel. The banquet room was filled with wedding guests, some dancing to the lilting music of the full orchestra, others filling dishes with exotic food from the buffet table, and here and there stood knots of people deep in discussion. Gina hugged Cindy and Bob, shook hands with Cindy's mother as she murmured a polite greeting, and kissed Stewart lightly on the cheek, uncomfortably aware of his ex-wife standing next to him.

His arms closed around her and he held her close as he murmured, "You can do better than that, darling. I'll be free in about fifteen minutes, save me a dance."

A uniformed waiter handed her a glass of champagne and she sipped the bubbly wine as her gaze wandered around the posh room, as lush as a garden with its innumerable potted plants, cut flower arrangements, and a wall of glass that provided a spectacular view of the ocean at dusk. Gina had lived in San Francisco for three years while her father was stationed at the Presidio and she'd loved it. She'd graduated from high school in the top ten percent of her class and had completed part of her freshman year of college before the debacle that sent her scurrying as far away as she could get, vowing never to return.

She wandered over to the glass wall and her memories were poignant and bittersweet as she stood looking out over the quaintly beautiful city of hills. She'd been standing there for several minutes when she became aware of an unfamiliar tension that had nothing to do with her thoughts. It was a tightening at the base of her skull, as though someone was blowing lightly on her neck, making the short hairs stand up. She shivered and looked over her shoulder. There were people all around but none of them were paying the slightest attention to her.

She moved unobtrusively to the long buffet table and picked up a silver fork and a china plate, but the uneasy feeling persisted and now she recognized it. It was the feeling of being watched intently. This time she turned and scanned the room, but the lighting was dim and everywhere she looked she saw expensively dressed, beautifully groomed strangers talking and laughing with each other. No one was staring at her and she mentally chided herself as she turned back to the table.

It was nerves, it had to be. Not only had the wedding unstrung her, but she hadn't eaten anything all day but a half-portion of crab salad at noon. She'd been drinking champagne on an empty stomach and she needed to eat something. Gina piled her plate with steaming, succulent gourmet food and carried it to a table where she spotted Twyla sitting with a similar plate before her. She had just raised a fork full of potatoes au gratin to her mouth when Gina approached.

Twyla lowered the filled fork and glared at Gina. "I

know what you're thinking so don't say it," she growled. "I solemnly swear to go back on my diet tomorrow, but tonight I'm not going to pass up any of this luscious fattening repast."

She popped the potatoes dripping with melted cheese sauce in her mouth and chewed blissfully.

Gina laughed as she took the seat beside her. "You nut, I don't care what you eat! They have strawberry cheesecake on the dessert table, would you like me to bring you a piece?"

"Oh, shut up and stop tempting me," groaned Twyla good-naturedly as she speared a batter-coated deep-fried oyster.

A hand on Gina's shoulder and a deep familiar voice caused her to look up. "Mind if I sit with you two?" Stewart asked as he put his plate on the table and sat down beside her. He sighed. "My feet are killing me and my arm aches. I've been standing in that receiving line forever and I think I've shaken hands with everyone in San Francisco."

Gina reached out and gently massaged the gray-coated shoulder. "Poor baby," she cooed as her fingers caressed him.

He smiled and put his hand over hers. "Just what I need, a twenty-five-year-old mother."

He drew her hand to his lips and kissed her palm as he murmured for her ears alone, "I have a mother and a daughter, sweetheart, but I badly need you for a wife."

Gina felt the flush rising to her face as she squeezed Stewart's hand and lowered her head. Without ever meaning to he had jabbed at her most vulnerable spot. She knew she was being unfair to him by procrastinating at setting a date for their own wedding. It had been four months since she had accepted his engagement ring and he had every right to expect her to make the final commitment soon. It wouldn't be so urgent if they were sleeping together, but they weren't. She still couldn't allow herself to become that intimately involved with a man, not even with Stewart.

They finished eating and Stewart asked Gina to dance. She snuggled against him as they moved gracefully in time to the waltz and her troubled thoughts returned.

It wasn't that she didn't love Stewart, she did. Oh, not with the passionate intensity that she had loved Peter Van Housen; that type of insanity was a one-time experience for the very young and for that she was deeply grateful. Her feelings for Stewart were quieter, more mature and, she was sure, more lasting.

He wanted her physically and let her know it. He may be in his forties but he was a virile, passionate man and he had a right as her fiancé to expect that they would make love. It was accepted behavior these days and in spite of her strict upbringing Gina did not disapprove. Stewart loved her, he wanted to marry her as soon as possible, and still she held him off. She wondered why he put up with her nonsense, but even as she wondered she knew. Because that's the kind of man he was, unselfish, patient and kind. He would never force her into a relationship she wasn't ready for, but wasn't she taking unfair advantage of his love?

The evening seemed to drag on interminably and at intervals she still had that eerie feeling of being watched, although she could never catch anyone staring at her. The cake had finally been cut and as soon as the photographer was finished taking pictures and the bridal couple had changed clothes they would leave and then Gina could go to her room and hide.

Hide! The word startled her. What on earth did she want to hide from?

Stewart was with the bridal party being photographed and Gina, standing alone watching the proceedings, again had the feeling that someone was watching her. *This is just plain stupid,* she thought as a shiver passed over her, *maybe I'm coming unglued.*

She accepted another crystal glass of champagne from one of the ever vigilant waiters and headed for the balcony. She needed to get out of there, breathe in some fresh air, and get hold of herself.

The soft breeze from the ocean was chilly on her bare arms but she hardly noticed as she wandered over to the waist-high parapet and gazed out into the darkness. Actually, it wasn't really dark after all. Above her a myriad of stars twinkled and glowed, and beneath her the bright lights of the city stretched out for miles. San Francisco, the old and the new, where slums coexisted with affluence, and sparkling steel and glass high-rise buildings overlooked dingy wooden turn-of-the-century row houses. There was an old song called "I Left My Heart in San Francisco," and that's what Gina had done, but her heart had been broken and bleeding and she was better off without it.

She was so lost in her reverie that she failed to hear the footsteps of the approaching man. Although the voice that spoke to her back was little more than a whisper she recognized it immediately.

"Hello, Ginny Lea."

Just three words, but a shock of such magnitude tore through her that the expensive glass slipped from her fingers and splintered on the tiles at her feet. She

jerked awkwardly as she turned and wondered, idioti-
cally, if Stewart would be charged for it.

Her gaze started at the firm hard jawline, moved
upward to the full sensual mouth, the nose with the
slight bump where it had once been broken, and
finally came to rest in the deep blue eyes of her
ex-husband, Peter Van Housen!

Chapter Two

It had been a long, emotional day and Gina was in no condition to sustain such a shattering encounter. She felt the color drain from her face and her whole body trembled.

Peter had aged. There were lines around his mouth and at the corners of his eyes that hadn't been there before, and his hair had darkened from platinum to wheat. He was still slender, but now it was almost a gauntness instead of boyish look.

She closed her eyes in an effort to block him out, to convince herself that she was hallucinating. The darkness unbalanced her and she swayed and would have fallen except for the arms that enfolded her against the familiar chest. For a moment she was totally incapable of resisting and leaned helplessly against the throbbing of his heartbeat. The musky smell of him assailed her nostrils and the finely spun wool of his blue suit coat rubbed against her cheek. She was shivering violently and his arms tightened as he buried his white face in her black, feathered hair.

A troubled male voice from behind them broke the spell.

"What's going on here?"

It was Stewart!

The sound of Stewart's voice brought Gina back to reality and she pulled swiftly away from Peter, then swayed as another wave of dizziness overcame her. This time it was Stewart who held her and he became thoroughly alarmed as she continued to tremble in his arms.

"Sweetheart," he said, his tone showing his concern. "What's the matter? Are you sick?"

Before she could answer, Twyla's voice sounded from her side. "Yes she is, Stewart, she was ill during the wedding ceremony but wouldn't admit it. I think we'd better get her upstairs to our room."

Stewart brushed a few tendrils of hair back from her pale face and spoke over her head to Peter, who was standing behind her now. "Sorry, Peter, can you tell me what happened?"

Gina stiffened. Stewart and Peter must know each other! Oh no, not that! Peter had just started to say something when she interrupted hastily. "I—I had a dizzy spell and Pete—Mr. Van Housen steadied me."

Steadied her! That was a laugh! Never, since the first time she saw him, had Peter Van Housen had a steadying effect on her. He'd garbled her thoughts and scrambled her brain until she couldn't think straight, and now after all this time he was doing it again.

Stewart was talking and she made an effort to concentrate on what he was saying. "I've been trying to introduce you two all evening but couldn't find you both at the same time. Now, apparently, someone's already done the honors. Well, Peter, what do you think of my girl?"

Gina straightened and turned to Peter, hoping to find a way to keep him from telling Stewart the truth. She might have been looking back in time. The expression on his face was the same one she had seen seven years ago, cold, hard and filled with disgust. There was a chill in his voice as he said, "You mean this is your *Gina?*"

Thank goodness for Twyla. The earth mother in her had taken over and she put a comforting arm around Gina's waist as she said, "You two can stand around all night and talk if you want to, but I'm going to take this poor child upstairs and put her to bed. She's apparently coming down with something."

Twyla started to lead Gina away when without a word Stewart swept her up in his arms and strode with her toward the elevator, leaving Peter standing there watching, his face shadowed and inscrutable.

Upstairs Stewart put Gina gently on one of the two queen-size beds in the room, and then reluctantly yielded to Twyla's demand that he go back down to his daughter's wedding reception and let Gina rest. He made Twyla promise that she'd call him if Gina couldn't sleep, then kissed Gina lingeringly, although she couldn't have responded if her life depended on it, and left.

Twyla closed and locked the door behind him, then turned and leaned against it as her glance sought Gina's. "Okay, baby, tell mama all about it."

Gina's eyes widened with surprise. "All—all about what?" she stammered.

Twyla strolled across the room and took a gold

cigarette case from her purse. "Gina, I'm neither stupid nor blind," she muttered with exasperation as she extracted a long slim cigarette from the case with two tropicana-red fingernails. "When you enrolled in my art class at the University of Maryland seven years ago you had just moved there from San Francisco and you were an emotional basket case. Today you're back in San Francisco and you're behaving very much like the heartbroken little Ginny Lea Brown you were then."

She put the cigarette between her lips and flicked the gold lighter she had also taken from her purse. The tip of the cigarette glowed as she inhaled deeply, then she clicked the top shut on the lighter and dropped it back in her purse.

"Except for saying that you'd had an unhappy love affair you've never told me what happened back then, and I've never asked. I figured when you wanted to tell me you would. Meanwhile, you've dropped the childish nickname, graduated from college with a degree in fine arts, and are fast becoming known as an outstanding young artist. You're no longer a teenager, Gina, you're a woman with an enviable record of successes behind you. You've overcome that devastating setback of seven years ago and you have a bright future ahead of you with a wonderful man."

She suddenly turned and faced Gina squarely. "In spite of all this, after spending less than twelve hours in San Francisco again you're back to being an emotional wreck. You're no more sick than I am. Something has shocked you right out of your mind and I want to know what it is. I'm asking you now, Gina, what happened here in San Francisco seven years ago that is still so painful that you can't face it?"

For a minute the room was so still that Gina could hear the almost-silent hum of the electric clock that sat on the bookcase in the headboard. For years now she had been underestimating Twyla Sisson. Gina had always known she was a talented artist, a smart businesswoman and teacher, and a dear supportive friend. But she hadn't realized that she was also a mind reader! Who else did she know who would have bothered to look past the obvious surface difficulty to find the deeper, more painful problem below?

A warm rush of gratitude swept over Gina, banishing a little of the icy chill that she thought had settled in her bones forever. She pulled herself up to a sitting position on the bed and ran her nervous fingers through her raven locks, then managed a wobbly smile at Twyla. "You're right, my nosy friend," she said gently. "It is time for me to talk about this. Are you sure you want to listen?"

Twyla grinned. "You know me, a combination of Mother Confessor and gossip columnist. You talk, I'll listen."

Gina swung her legs over the side of the bed and kicked off her shoes. "Okay," she said with a sigh, "but do you mind if I shower first and get into something comfortable? I've got to calm myself down a little." She held out her hand. "Look, my hands are still shaking."

Twyla nodded. "Go ahead, and while you're showering I'll call room service and have a pot of coffee sent up. It promises to be a long night."

When Gina emerged from the bathroom fifteen minutes later wrapped in a white terrycloth robe she saw that Twyla had also changed into a tawny gold satin nightgown and matching peignoir. A silver coffee service and two pink china cups sat on the tea table in the corner of the room, and Gina shook her head as she filled the two fragile cups with the steaming, fragrant liquid. "I've never been in such a luxurious hotel before," she said. "The ones I've stayed in had a small hot pot with little envelopes of instant coffee and paper cups in a plastic holder." She handed Twyla one of the china cups. "I'll bet this room is costing Stewart a fortune."

Twyla snorted. "The whole wedding's costing Stewart a fortune! He'll probably have to write an extra book just to pay for it. Cindy and Bob would have been a lot smarter if they'd taken the money and eloped to Reno."

Gina sat down in the soft blue-velvet-upholstered chair that was a twin to the one Twyla was lounging in. "Shame on you, Twyla," she teased. "Haven't you any romance in your soul?"

Twyla set her cup and saucer on the lamp table that separated their two chairs. "Nope," she declared. "I gave up on romance when my husband ran off with a nineteen-year-old girl and left me with over fifty thousand dollars worth of his debts to pay off. Since then I only place my trust in cold hard cash."

Gina set her cup and saucer beside Twyla's. "I'm sorry," she said softly, "I didn't know."

Twyla shrugged. "So we all have problems, but it's yours we're going to talk about tonight. Let's get on with it. My question was, what happened here seven years ago that can still upset you so badly?"

Gina took a deep breath and answered. "I got married."

"Married!" Twyla gasped.

Gina nodded. "Yes, in a ceremony very much like

the one today. That's why I was so upset. The memories—"

"But—but how long did this marriage last? I assume you're single now?"

Gina felt the tension that she had washed away under the hot shower rising in her again. "The marriage was made in heaven at high noon and ended in hell four hours later. It was annulled without ever being consummated."

"Good Heaven!" Twyla's brown eyes were wide with astonishment. "You poor child. You couldn't have been more than seventeen at the time."

Gina sighed. "I was eighteen, a freshman in college, and the future was bright and beautiful and mine for the taking. I'd always sketched, and painted, and shaped things with clay, but then I was enrolled in the fine arts program and I was going to be the world's first female Michaelangelo. Instead I met—Peter Van Housen."

"Peter Van Housen!" Twyla all but screamed. "You mean *the* Peter Van Housen, director of the most prestigious private art gallery in the bay area?"

Gina nodded. "The same. Only then he was just the youngest son of Hans Van Housen, millionaire financier and art fancier. Their art collection was housed in their mansion in the Seacliff area and was viewed only by invitation. I understand they built the new gallery on Maiden Lane and opened it to the public about three years later."

She picked up her cup and saucer and sipped at the still warm coffee. "I met Peter when my art class took a tour of the famed Van Housen art collection. We were studying Dutch artists at the time and they had an excellent collection of van Goghs, Rembrandts,

Jan Steens and Vermeers. Peter had chosen to be our guide that day because the Dutch collection was his special area of expertise. So help me it was a classic case of love at first sight."

Gina took the last swallow of her coffee and set the cup and saucer aside. She gave a short, mirthless laugh. "Oh how trusting are the young! It sounds silly when I try to talk about it, especially in the light of what happened less than two months later, but there was something magical in the feeling that sprang to life between us.

"He was a stranger. I didn't even know he existed when I woke up that morning, but by nightfall the whole direction of my life had changed. I'd come under the spell of a man eight years older than I but light-years older in experience, and from then on no one could deter me from my dream, the dream of spending all eternity in the arms of Peter Van Housen.

"He kept me close to him that afternoon but I didn't see a picture or hear a word he said. He claimed later that he didn't remember what he said either. Before I left he asked for my address and phone number, and from that time on we were together every spare minute."

"Now wait a minute," interrupted Twyla. "Surely it wasn't as idyllic as all that."

"Idyllic?" murmured Gina. "Of course not. We had opposition right from the start. My parents were concerned and his were furious! Mom and Dad tried to tell me that I was way out of my depth, that Peter was too old, too rich, and too sophisticated for me, and at first the Van Housens didn't even take me seriously. They treated me like a mongrel pup their spoiled son had brought home and insisted on keeping. They tolerated me only because they were sure he'd soon cast me aside for the show dog he already had."

"Hold it," interrupted Twyla holding up a hand. "Are you telling me you lived with this man in his parents' home?"

"No," snapped Gina. "That's not what I'm telling you! I was just trying to be cute because if I delve too deeply into this hellish experience I'm not going to be able to talk about it at all.

"When Peter first introduced me to his parents they were polite but totally uninterested because they had plans for their young son to marry the daughter of State Senator Frederick Miller. Her name was Veronica and she was all they could possibly want in a daughter-in-law—snobbish, rich, and well-connected. They assumed Peter was having a last fling with one of the local peasantry before settling down to marriage and family life."

"And was he?" Twyla said. "Having a 'fling' I mean."

Gina sniffed. "If you mean 'affair' the answer is no. My parents had strong moral values and they'd taught me well. I was convinced that it was wrong to go to bed with a man before the wedding vows and until I met Peter it had never been a problem. None of the boys I'd gone out with had attracted me in that way, although Mel was beginning to make some headway."

"Who's Mel?" questioned Twyla.

"Mel was Melvin Calicutt, a photography student whom I had been dating before I met Peter. We had a lot of fun together and he was pretty upset when I quit seeing him and started spending all my time with Peter."

She spread her hands and lowered her voice as though speaking to herself. "At the time I didn't realize just how upset he really was."

Twyla was watching her closely. "So you didn't sleep with Peter before the wedding?"

Gina winced and closed her eyes and tried to block out the memories Twyla's question evoked. Peter's eyes, smoky with passion; his hands making love to her breasts, her hips, her thighs; his lips teasing, clinging, possessing until she was aflame with desire. It had been agony to pull away, to hold him off, to tell him no.

With a supreme effort she dragged her thoughts back to the present. "No," she said in answer to the question. "We must have quarreled at least half a dozen times over my refusals. He'd call me a tease, a professional virgin, and roar away in his high-powered Mercedes, and I'd spend the night in tears, sure that this time I'd lost him, but he always came back. We couldn't stay apart, the attraction between us was too strong.

"Finally after two weeks of that he asked me to marry him, and I was sure that no woman in all of time had ever been so happy."

Gina shifted restlessly in her chair and ran her slender, coral-tipped fingers through her short hair. "I was too young, naïve, and blindly in love to understand that he was only marrying me because he couldn't get me in bed any other way."

Twyla gasped. "Oh come now Gina, you can't really believe that! Men don't marry reticent women anymore, they simply toss them over and find one who is more willing. If a man like Peter Van Housen married you over the objections of both sets of parents, then I'm betting that he loved you."

Gina covered her face with her hands and leaned her head back against the cushioned chair. "I don't know, Twyla." Her voice had an edge of despair. "I've been over it so often and I just don't know. Except for the times when I drove him half out of his mind with sexual frustration, he was always very gentle and loving with me. When we told his family we were going to be married they were horrified. He had two older brothers and a sister, all married, and not one of them took our side. They accused me of wanting only the Van Housen money and prestige, they reminded him that he was expected to marry Veronica Miller, his parents even threatened to disinherit him but none of it had any effect on us. We had to be together."

Twyla mashed out the stub of another cigarette in the modernistic ceramic ashtray and she sounded impatient as she said, "If you were both so wildly in love then for heaven's sake what happened?"

Gina took her hands from her face and looked at her friend. "We got married, that's what happened," she said bitterly. "Peter was the youngest son of a very rich man and he was pampered and indulged, used to having his own way. In the end his parents grudgingly withdrew their opposition and insisted that if there was going to be a wedding it would be done in the usual Van Housen tradition. Our hasty marriage was the social event of the season. Bertha Van Housen orchestrated it and Hans paid for it, and I'm sure everyone in San Francisco thought I was pregnant. I was seldom even consulted but I didn't mind. All I wanted was to get it over with so Peter and I could make love."

Twyla once more rummaged through her purse for the gold case and extracted a cigarette. She held it firmly between her lips as she searched for the lighter, then lit it and set the lighter on the table beside her. She inhaled deeply and slowly released the smoke into the air. "Gina," she said gratingly, "are you deliberately tormenting me? I want to know why this marriage that you say was made in heaven ended after only four hours."

A short, hollow laugh escaped Gina. "Maybe you're right, my friend. I guess I am deliberately holding back, but you see the part that comes next is so agonizing for me that even now I can hardly bring myself to face it."

She took a deep breath and forced herself to continue. "The reception was held at the Van Housen mansion where a huge tent was set up on the spacious grounds and a catered dinner was served. It seemed to go on forever, but finally Peter and I managed to break away and change our clothes. By then most of the guests had left and we were coming down the winding stairway with our families and attendants on our way to the car and freedom at last when the doorbell rang and a man insisted on seeing Peter.

"He turned out to be a special messenger with a large brown manila envelope for Peter. He was very upset, said the envelope was to have been delivered before noon, but he'd been involved in a three-car pileup on one of the bridges and was delayed more than three hours. The messenger stressed that he'd been told the parcel was extremely important, so Peter excused us and led me into the den where we could have some privacy while he examined the contents."

Again Gina twisted uncomfortably in her chair, fighting the memories that threatened to overpower her.

The examination of the contents of the parcel hadn't been the only thing for which Peter wanted privacy. As soon as the door had closed behind them he had taken her in his arms and his mouth had descended on hers, warm and eager and hungry. It was the first time they'd been alone together all day and she'd responded with an eagerness and a hunger that matched his.

For a long moment they were lost in the heat of their all-consuming desire, but then Peter pulled his lips from hers and groaned, "Why did I ever agree to drive all the way to Carmel to start our honeymoon? I don't think I can wait three more hours to make love to you."

His mouth once more found hers and his hands moved to her hips and arched her soft, pliant body into the hardness of his own. She'd shivered with the sensations of pleasure that were building in her, pleasure almost too intense to be borne. Her arms tightened around his neck as she strained to press herself even closer and she forgot everything but her burning need to be one with him.

A sharp rap on the door jolted them out of their steamy preoccupation and Peter muttered an oath as they pulled apart, somewhat disoriented. A voice filled with laughter had shouted, "Hey you two, don't start something it's going to take too long to finish. Everyone's waiting to send you off. . . ."

A hand on Gina's arm and a gentle shake brought her back to the present. "Honey," said Twyla in a worried tone, "if this is going to be too painful—"

Gina breathed deeply and shook her head. "No, I'm all right. Sorry, I was just—just trying to put my thoughts in order," she lied.

"Peter closed the door to the den and locked it,"

she continued, "then walked over to the desk while I stood back.

"I didn't immediately notice his startled reaction as he removed the contents of the envelope. When I finally became aware of the prolonged silence I looked up to see him standing at the desk in a stiff, unnatural stance with his back to me."

Gina felt hot and knew that her skin had a fine sheen of perspiration, but her hands were cold as she clasped them together in her lap. "The oddest sense of foreboding came over me at that moment and I shivered. *Someone walked over my grave,* I thought, then giggled nervously at the inappropriateness of the saying that was one of my grandmother's favorite expressions. This was my wedding day, the happiest day of my life.

"I forced myself to smile and started across the room toward Peter, curious about what could be in the slim envelope that was important enough to be sent by special messenger."

Suddenly the effort to sit still was more than Gina could bear and she stood up and began pacing around the room, her hands still clasped in front of her, her voice remaining clear and steady.

"I stood beside him and he turned and looked down at me. What I saw in his face made me gasp and step back, bewildered. The gentle, adoring lover was gone and in his place was a man of ice. His complexion was white, totally drained of color and his blue eyes were lifeless with shock. I—I asked him what was the matter and then my gaze shifted to his hands. The brown envelope had dropped to the desk and he was holding a large shiny piece of black and white paper, a photograph."

Gina stopped her pacing and stood still, trying to control the trembling that had overtaken her. She wondered if she could continue, if she should continue. It was tearing her apart, and for what purpose? Twyla couldn't help, nobody could. Wasn't it better not to delve into the past?

"Gina?" Twyla's soft question reached her and Gina knew she would go on, would finish the story she'd started. Twyla was a caring, compassionate lady and Gina was sure she'd need all the help she could get in the days to come. She had no doubt that what had happened tonight was a beginning, not an ending.

She straightened her shoulders and breathed a silent prayer for strength. "Peter didn't speak or move," she continued, "And those cold dead eyes seemed to bore into my very soul. My mouth felt dry and I ran the tip of my tongue over my lips as I begged him to tell me what was the matter.

"The photograph fluttered to the desk and a look of rage replaced the shock as he turned to fully face me. For a minute I was afraid he'd hit me, but then when he spoke I almost wished he had."

She resumed her pacing. "His voice was low but harsh, raspy, almost painful as he said, 'So my parents and Veronica were right, all you wanted from me was money and prestige. You lying, cheating little—!' The name he called me was gross, shocking, and I gasped as his powerful hands clamped my shoulders in a crushing grip. I can still hear him say, 'I could kill you, right here, this instant, with my bare hands!'

"He shook me until I was sure my neck would snap and I screamed with terror. The noise seemed to jar him into a semblance of reality and he released me so quickly that I lost my balance and fell to the floor. I lay there stunned, trembling with fear, as he strode across the room and unlocked the door, then disappeared down the hall."

Gina shivered and pulled her robe closer around her as she wondered why she seemed to be cold one minute and too warm the next. She hugged her arms across her chest as she continued to roam around the room.

"After that," she said, "everything seemed to be happening at once. My parents were bending over me, helping me to my feet, demanding to know what happened, while the rest of the wedding party apparently followed after Peter.

"I couldn't explain what happened because I didn't know, and it was several minutes before I remembered the photograph. The picture! It had to be something in the picture that turned Peter into a madman!

"It lay where it had fallen on the desk and I picked it up and looked at it, then blinked and looked again. It was an eight-by-ten glossy black and white portrait of Mel Calicutt and me. It was cropped at my waist and Mel's chest and arms were bare, and the only garment I was wearing was an unfastened black bra with straps that were sliding off my shoulders. We were in what appeared to be a passionately erotic embrace!"

Chapter Three

Gina stood in front of the wide window and parted the sheer draperies slightly so she could look out. She'd never been this high up in a building before, and even in the darkness the view was astounding. To the south were lights extending all the way down the peninsula, but to the west the illumination blended into darkness as it mingled with the vastness of the ocean.

From behind her Twyla's husky voice broke the silence. "Well, was it?"

"Was it what?" Gina asked without turning.

"Was it a passionate embrace someone caught you in with Mel Calicutt, or was the picture faked?"

Gina leaned her forehead against the cool glass. "It was neither, and don't ever let anyone tell you that photos don't lie. At first I was stunned. There had never been anything sexual between Mel and me. We'd had a friendly easy relationship and shared a few goodnight kisses but that was all. I hadn't gone out with him since I'd met Peter."

She straightened then and turned to look at Twyla.

"It was several minutes before I finally remembered when that picture must have been taken. Mel and I were in the same photography class, that's where we met. One day about a week before the wedding our teacher announced that he had made arrangements for us to go by bus to an estate in Marin County where we would be allowed to photograph the inside of the fabulous home. He told us to bring our bathing suits because we would be allowed to swim in the indoor pool. It was January and none of us had been to the beach in months so we were all delighted with the extra bonus."

Gina walked over and sat back down in the chair beside Twyla. "It was a fabulous day. Some of the art treasures in that home were priceless and Mel and I paired off and worked together photographing them. About mid-afternoon we were given permission to swim, and I changed into the new black bikini I'd bought for my trousseau. It was really quite modest for a bikini, the top was a bra style with straps and the bottom was a slip-on pantie that pulled up nearly to my waist. Mel appeared in brief trunks, and after we'd been in the pool for a while he suggested we have a glass of the punch that was being served."

She frowned as she continued. "I remember now that he led me around behind a huge tropical plant that seemed to be growing right out of the tiles and we sat on our towels on the floor. Mel began acting strange, telling me how desirable I looked, touching my hand, running his fingers up my arm. I didn't want to make a scene so I tried to ignore it, but suddenly he grabbed me and kissed me, passionately. I was so surprised that for a moment I just leaned against him as his hands roamed, but I quickly came to my senses and started to fight. He wouldn't let me go. Then, as suddenly as it started it was over. He released me and apologized, but I didn't appreciate being mauled and told him so. I got dressed and didn't speak to him again. If he came to the wedding I didn't see him. When I saw the picture I realized someone must have photographed us in that impromptu embrace. My bikini top had gotten disheveled during the scuffle and the look on my face which was really surprise photographed as wanton passion."

Twyla's voice was questioning as she spoke. "But surely you could have explained that to Peter."

Gina shrugged. "You'd think so, wouldn't you? Unfortunately there was also a note enclosed with the picture. It was typewritten and unsigned and said, 'Thought you should know what your sweet, virginal bride-to-be is doing when you're not around.'"

"That's rotten!" exploded Twyla.

Gina didn't comment, but once more picked up her story. "I didn't see Peter again for two days when my dad and some of his army buddies finally found him passed out in a sleazy bar. When we got him sobered up I tried to explain about the incident leading up to the taking of the picture. He wasn't having any of it. He kept insisting that his parents and Veronica were right all along, that I saw a chance to marry into wealth and social position and took advantage of his strong physical attraction for me to maneuver him into proposing by playing the pure virgin who couldn't let him make love to me until we were married."

Unable to sit still Gina stood and poured herself another cup of coffee, then left it sitting on the tray, forgotten. "I was so incredibly naïve and stupid in those days. I knew that Peter was well aware that there were always people anxious to take advantage of the very wealthy. He'd told me once that both of his brothers had unhappy love affairs with women who were only after their money and social position before they finally married women who were as wealthy as they, but I still didn't see the trap. I was so sure that if he would just go with me to talk to Mel everything would be all right. That Mel would back up my story and Peter would know that I was innocent as I'd told him I was."

"It didn't turn out that way, I gather?" muttered Twyla.

"You'd better believe it didn't!" Gina's voice was filled with self-derision. "I walked right into it, just the way I was set up to. Peter finally agreed to talk to Mel, and I called and made arrangements to meet him at his apartment.

"We showed him the picture and the note. He looked at them, then at me, and I can quote his exact words. He said, "Sorry, sweetheart, I had no idea we were being observed on that secluded stretch of beach. We should have been more careful, but surely Peter knows we've been—uh—going together."

Twyla sat straight and gripped the arms of her chair. "That bastard!" she hissed.

"Agreed," said Gina. "Peter hit him and knocked him across the room, then tore up the picture and slammed out of the apartment without even a glance at me. I never saw him again until tonight."

"Tonight!" Twyla exclaimed. "You saw Peter Van Housen tonight?"

Gina looked at her, puzzled. "Of course, you were there, you saw the state of collapse I was in . . ."

She stopped as she realized that in all the confusion Twyla probably hadn't been introduced to Peter.

"You mean," Twyla demanded, "that the man who

was holding you as though he'd never let you go was your ex-husband? I've met Peter Van Housen a time or two, but I'm afraid I wasn't paying any attention to him tonight. I was too concerned about you."

Gina caught her breath and hissed, "Don't be such a romantic, Twyla. He wasn't holding me, he was merely propping me up so I wouldn't faint at his feet."

"That's not the way it looked to me, or to Stewart either." Her eyes narrowed. "Does Stewart know you were married to Peter Van Housen?"

Gina shook her head. "No. He thinks like you did that I had an unhappy teenage love affair. I didn't see any point in mentioning a marriage that was never in fact a marriage at all."

"Did you know that Stewart and Peter were acquainted?"

"Good heavens no!" sputtered Gina. "I'd never have come here today if I had. Not that it really matters. I understand that after the annulment Peter married Veronica and they spend most of their time in Europe ferreting out art treasures for the gallery."

"Where did you hear that?" Twyla asked doubtfully.

Gina shrugged, trying to act nonchalant, as if even now remembering that small bit of gossip wasn't like twisting the knife in an already mortal wound. "I overheard a couple of artists discussing the Van Housen gallery shortly after I came back to the West Coast three years ago and they happened to mention it."

"Did you ever find out why Mel did such a monstrous thing?" Twyla asked.

"Oh yes," Gina answered. "After Peter stomped out I was wildly hysterical. I screamed, threw things, and beat at Mel with my fists. When he finally got me calmed down he readily admitted what he'd done. He said that Veronica Miller, the woman who had thought she was going to marry Peter, had found out about Mel's heavy gambling debts and offered to pay them if he would arrange to have an incriminating picture made of the two of us. She arranged the picture-taking session for the class at her uncle's estate and supplied the hidden photographer. All Mel had to do was make love to me for a few minutes and then develop the film and arrange for a messenger to deliver it and the note to Peter just before the wedding. Unfortunately for Veronica the messenger was delayed, but she accomplished her purpose. A few days later Peter's lawyer came to me with papers to sign agreeing to an annulment."

Gina slumped down on the side of her bed and fought the sobs she felt rising in her throat. Her voice shook as she continued. "Mel's last words to me were, 'I didn't want to hurt you, baby, but I was in to those guys for several thou' and they don't take credit cards.' He left town a few days later, and I finally faced the grim reality. If Peter had so little faith in my goodness and honesty then the marriage wouldn't have lasted anyway. It was better that it had never begun."

The sobs could no longer be held back, and she dropped her head in her hands and let the tears, that had been pressing behind her eyes, flow. With a strangled sound Twyla jumped up and knelt before her. She wrapped her arms around Gina's convulsive form and murmured comforting endearments as she rocked her back and forth. "Gina, honey," she soothed, "do you still love Peter so much?"

Gina's voice was wracked with sobs as she wailed, "You—you don't understand. My—my love for him di—died years ago. I—I hate him and I hope I—I never see him again as—as long as I live."

"Sure you do," Twyla murmured in a tone of disbelief.

Monday morning dawned bright and warm in the renowned artist colony of Mendocino, California, with just a wisp of a breeze from the ocean to keep the July sun from becoming too hot. Gina pulled on her white jeans, tugged a red- and white-striped blouse over her head and pulled it down to just below her tiny waist. It had a nautical collar at the back and red laces that crisscrossed the six-inch slit at the neckline in front. She found her red espadrilles and slipped her feet into them as she fought back conflicting feelings of anticipation and dread.

Peter was coming. Maybe not today, or tomorrow, but he would come. She knew it in her bones, and in her flesh, and in the soft beat of her heart. She wasn't looking forward to it; if there was any way she could avoid him she would, but this meeting was inevitable. She knew now that it had to take place before she could truly relate to any other man, before she could give herself wholeheartedly to Stewart Tobias.

Saturday had been a nightmare and Twyla, bless her, had at last tucked Gina into bed and given her a liberal dose of a tranquilizer that caused her to sleep deeply. She was wakened on Sunday morning by a concerned Stewart, and it hadn't been difficult to convince him they should start home for Mendocino immediately. They'd lost no time in checking out of the luxurious high-rise hotel and making their way across the Golden Gate Bridge then north to Highway 1, the narrow, winding road that hugs the ruggedly beautiful northern California coastline.

Stewart had been inclined to make a leisurely day of the drive, but Gina couldn't leave San Francisco behind fast enough and urged him not to tarry. Twyla remained neutral. They stopped only once, at Bodega Bay, for breakfast, and arrived home to Mendocino in time for a late lunch.

It was during that trip, while Twyla kept the conversation going with Stewart, that Gina managed to set her thoughts in order. She realized now that she had just been marking time with her life, that the shock of the abrupt disintegration of her marriage had left her in a state of suspended animation. She couldn't give herself to another man until she'd brought her relationship with Peter full circle and healed the wound that was still raw.

Gina plugged in the automatic coffee maker and strolled out onto the balcony that ran the width of her second floor apartment. She never tired of the sight or the sound of the small bay just across Main Street and down a slight embankment. It was so peaceful, and in times of stress she came out here to lean against the railing and watch the sunbeams playing on the blue-green water, or the white waves splashing against the rocky shore. By noon the deserted streets below would be alive with tourists, artists, art lovers and collectors who during the summer swarm to this quaint Cape Cod-type village with its ancient clapboard houses, converted now into small independent art galleries and boutiques.

Gina checked the gold jeweled watch Stewart had given her for Christmas. Before long she would have to go downstairs and open her own gallery, known simply as "Gina's," that comprised the entire lower floor of this house. Gina worked on the ground level, lived on the top level, and made regular payments to the mortgage company.

She stepped back through the glass doors into the long living room that fronted the house. At the west end a round walnut table and two matching chairs provided a dining area that blended in with the somewhat meager furnishings of the rest of the room. When Gina occasionally entertained it was very informal, usually a buffet dinner with over-sized cushions for the majority of the guests who preferred to sit on the floor, and T.V. trays for the rest.

The old-fashioned kitchen opened off the dining area. Gina poured herself a cup of coffee and was rummaging through the elderly refrigerator looking for an orange when the melodious tones of organ music chimed softly through the house. The doorbell. Another gift from Stewart who hated the raucous scream most of them made.

Now who could that be this early in the morning? she thought, then, remembering the art supplies she'd ordered the previous week, decided it was a delivery man. "Just a minute," she called as she hurried to the small entry hall on the east side of the house and fumbled with the lock before opening the door.

Her breath caught in her throat and her violet eyes widened as she clutched the doorknob and stared at the tall blond man who stood on the landing at the top of her outdoor stairway. It was Peter, looking as sexy as he ever had in custom-tailored brown slacks that fit tightly around his slender waist and hips and revealed the muscular firmness of his thighs. His shirt was terra-cotta and tan with a touch of lemon, worn open at the neck and topped with a lightweight beige, V-necked slipover sweater.

"May I come in?" he asked in that husky, sensuous voice that always had sent shivers down her spine. This time was no exception, and she heard the slight tremor in her voice as she said, "Yes, of course, please do," and stepped aside so he could enter.

He brushed against her lightly in the narrow passageway and she wondered if he could hear the pounding of her heart. *This is ridiculous,* she told herself. *Peter Van Housen means nothing to me anymore! My stupid emotions are unsettled because I didn't expect him to come so early in the morning.*

He walked into the living room without waiting to be directed, and as she followed behind she wondered if her trembling legs would continue to hold her up. "Won't you sit down?" she said politely, as though he were a stranger who had come to call. She motioned to the comfortable but inexpensive russet- and cream-striped sofa. "I'll get you some coffee."

She turned and made her way quickly to the kitchen, but escape wasn't going to be that easy. This time *he* had followed *her* and was standing behind her as her shaking hands poured more coffee on the counter than they did in the cup. Peter muttered an oath as he took the glass coffee pitcher from her and set it back on the heating element, then picked up both their cups and carried them to the pine kitchen table that was covered with a red- and white-checked cloth.

It was apparent to Gina that he wasn't affected by this meeting. He was calm and cool and treating her like an overwrought child. They sat across from each other at the table and she could find no trace of emotion in either his strong, handsome face or his deep blue eyes, those eyes that had once leaped with a fiery passion when they looked at her. Well that's the way she wanted it, she told herself. He'd never really loved her, and now he was married to Veronica and they probably had several children, although she couldn't visualize the super-sophisticated Veronica changing diapers or kissing little faces smeared with puréed vegetables.

She took a deep breath and hoped her voice wouldn't quiver as she said, "Why are you here, Peter?"

He raised a dark brown eyebrow. "Surely you aren't going to tell me you weren't expecting me."

She took a sip of coffee and tried again. "I suppose Stewart told you where I live?"

"Well I sure as hell didn't find out from you!" he exploded. "Where have you been for the last seven years, Ginny Lea?"

So there was some emotion under that cold exterior. He might be human after all. "I—my father asked for temporary duty on the east coast and was sent to Maryland. I graduated from the university there four years later and was offered a job here in Mendocino. I came and stayed."

He glared at her. "You mean you've been here for three years?" he said gratingly.

She nodded. "My friend, Twyla Sisson, who was an art teacher of mine at the University of Maryland, was left a small legacy by an elderly relative. She came out here and bought half-interest in Gallery By The Sea, which is our most prestigious art gallery—"

He waved her explanation aside absently. "I'm familiar with Gallery By The Sea and I've heard of Twyla Sisson. Is she the reason you came out here?"

"Yes," answered Gina, "she sent me a plane ticket for a graduation present, and I decided to stay here and work for her. After a while I started selling some of my own paintings too, and eventually I bought this place. The gallery is on the floor below."

"I know," Peter said. "I looked through the windows before I came upstairs." He looked straight at her. "You must not have lived with Mel long."

She gasped. There it was, the taunting, hateful thrust. She'd known it was coming, but not when, or how. Peter was still watching her and she wasn't going to let him see how badly he still had the power to hurt her. "I haven't seen Mel since the day you and I went to talk to him," she said simply.

There was emotion in his face now. It was disbelief tinged with disgust. "Don't lie to me," he snapped. "I returned to San Francisco after a few weeks and both you and Mel were gone. I was told you'd left together."

It didn't take much imagination to know who told him that! Well, there was no sense in arguing about it, he wouldn't believe her anyway. "It doesn't matter to me anymore what you believe, Peter. Did you just come here to torment me?"

"Torment *you!*" he hissed. "I couldn't even begin to dish out the kind of torment you seem to have mastered. Don't forget, my passionate little artist, that *I* was the injured party in that long-ago calamity." He nearly toppled his chair as he stood and turned away from her. "How I could ever have been so gullible—"

He stood there for a moment, tense and silent, and Gina clasped her shaking hands together in her lap. She wondered if she was strong enough to withstand a replay of those dreadful scenes she'd had with Peter seven years ago. Why, oh why had she ever come back to California? She'd known at the time that it was probably a mistake, but she never seemed to learn—

Peter's voice broke into her thoughts and it was once again cool and controlled. "How long have you been engaged to Stewart Tobias?"

Gina breathed a sigh of relief. He wasn't going to pursue the old argument after all. She answered his question almost eagerly. "I met him shortly after I came here, and we've been engaged about four months."

He turned toward her and leaned against the wall. "When are you planning to be married?"

There was an undercurrent to his tone, and Gina stiffened. "We—we haven't set a date yet."

"Why aren't you living with him?"

The question and the manner in which it was asked touched a spring in her nervous system and she jumped to her feet and faced him. "That's none of your business!" she rasped. "You have no right to pry into my personal relationship with Stewart!"

His hands gripped her shoulders before she could see them coming and move away. "The hell I haven't!" he shouted. "You married *me*, remember?"

The nerve of him! The unmitigated gall! She tried to twist away from him, but his fingers dug into her flesh as he hauled her closer.

She pushed against his chest with the palms of her hands as she cried, "That was never a marriage and you know it! You couldn't wait to take advantage of what looked like an excuse to end it, and your lawyer came around two days later with annulment papers and made it official. Now get out of here. Go home to your wife and leave me alone!''

His painful grip on her shoulders loosened and a look of surprise crossed his face. "Wife?" he exclaimed.

"Yes, wife." She tried again to pull away but he held her firm. "Did you think I hadn't heard that you married Veronica after the annulment? Or that the two of you live most of the time in Europe? Had you forgotten that art circles have sharp grapevines?''

All emotion drained from his features and they settled into an impenetrable mask. "Veronica's dead," he said coldly. "She was killed two years ago in a skiing accident in Switzerland."

A wave of horror swept through Gina, melting the rage that had built up within her. Veronica dead. That beautiful, willful woman who had all the advantages life could give. She'd been vicious and Gina had hated her, but she'd never wished her dead! And Peter. What had Veronica's death done to him?

She realized that she'd been staring at him without really seeing him. In an instinctive gesture she reached up and touched his cheek with her fingers. A muscle twitched in his jaw as she whispered, "Oh Peter, I'm so sorry."

His hands left her shoulders and his arms encircled her waist as he cradled her against his tall lean body and rubbed the cheek with the rough contour of his jaw. "So am I," he murmured.

For a long moment they stood silently embracing, their bodies moving together as one. She could feel his heart beating in rhythm with her own, and the tangy scent of citrus shaving lotion blended with his own warm maleness to produce a highly sensual aroma that stirred repressed longings deep inside her.

Peter was the first to break the spell. "Why didn't you answer my letters, Ginny Lea?"

She pushed away from him and this time he let her go. "What letters?"

"When I returned to San Francisco and found you gone I wrote to you at your parents' last address and asked that it be forwarded," he explained. "I know you received the letter because I never got it back, but you never answered it."

Gina ran her hand through her raven locks in a gesture of frustration. Was there no end to the evils he could think up to accuse her of? Was he still bent on punishing her for her so-called sins? Well, she wasn't going to let him do that. She was a big girl now. She'd grown up in the last seven years. She was no longer eighteen, wildly in love, and quiveringly vulnerable. He could only hurt her now if she let him, and that she would not do.

She took a deep breath and replied. "I didn't answer your nonexistent letter because I never received it. Don't lie to me, Peter, I'm not stupid. We left a forwarding address at the post office. If you'd mailed a letter to me I would have gotten it."

Peter's light skin flushed darkly and his fists clenched and unclenched at his sides. "Hell, woman," he roared. "Don't you ever admit to any of your wrongdoings? And you have the brass to stand there and call *me* a liar! I not only wrote to you once, but after a couple of weeks when I received no reply I wrote again. Now don't try to tell me you didn't get either letter because that's just too much of a coincidence. One lost in the mail, maybe. Two, never."

Gina sank wearily down on the chair she had recently vacated. "This is getting us nowhere, Peter," she said tonelessly. "Please, just leave. Go back to

San Francisco or Europe or wherever it is that you live and leave me alone."

In a move that caught her by surprise Peter hunkered down in front of her and put a hand on either side of her waist. His blue eyes looked deeply into her violet ones. "But I can't leave you alone, Ginny Lea," he murmured roughly and pulled her forward so she slid off the chair and onto her knees on the floor.

Before she could protest his mouth covered hers in a hard punishing kiss. Her lips parted in a gasp admitting his seeking, plundering tongue. She struggled, pounding her fists on his back, but his arms tightened around her waist, pulling her between his thighs, making her aware of his taut, hard muscles and the urgency of his need for her. Her body ignited like dry straw under a torch and it was as it had been years ago, only more so. With a moan of surrender her arms clasped around his neck and she pressed even closer in a frenzied desire to assuage his male needs and to ease the burning ache in her own body.

Their lovemaking was so intense that she was totally unprepared when he suddenly unclasped her arms from around him and pushed her away. His breath was coming in short rasping pants as he stood and looked down at her bewildered upturned face.

"Oh no, Ginny Lea," he said, "I can't leave you alone because you belong to me. I never filed those annulment papers. Like it or not you're still my wife and you can forget any plans you've made to marry Stewart Tobias!"

He turned quickly and walked out of the house, slamming the door behind him, and she could hear his heavy footsteps on every one of the eighteen wooden steps before he reached the sidewalk.

His wife! Peter had said she was still his wife! Oh please, no!

Gina sat back on her heels and buried her ravaged face in her hands as dry sobs shook her slender frame. Once more Peter Van Housen had brought her to her knees and her defenses against him had been as effective as a sprinkling can at an inferno!

Chapter Four

The sun was still shining brightly at seven o'clock but Gina had wilted long before then. Her head ached from the effort she'd put into concentrating on the business of answering her customers' interminable questions and now and then selling them a picture or a small, relatively inexpensive sculpture. Usually she loved the tourists with their inquisitive expressions, their bubbling laughter and their bulging wallets, but today her nerves were rubbed raw and her hand was unsteady as she fitted the key in the lock of the gallery door.

A voice from behind made her jump. "I've been waiting for you to lock up. Come, I'll take you to dinner."

She closed her eyes for a moment in an effort to ease the pounding in her head and regain her composure, then turned to face Peter Van Housen. She should have known he'd do the unexpected. All day long she'd jumped every time the little bell signaled the opening of the door. She'd known he would return but she'd expected him earlier, not now when she'd finally let down her guard and was confident of reprieve.

She dropped her key in her purse and sighed. "Not tonight, Peter, I haven't the stamina for another encounter with you. Perhaps tomorrow."

He took her arm and started to walk with her. "You'll feel better once you've had a drink. We'll go to the Mendocino Lodge. I'll have dinner sent up to my room and we can talk."

He stopped in front of a sleek, shiny black Jaguar and leaned down to open the door on the passenger side. She pulled away from him angrily. "I'm not going to your room with you. Call me tomorrow and we'll arrange something more public."

She tried to brush past him but his fingers clamped around her wrist. "Grow up, Ginny Lea," he snapped. "That virginal innocence routine doesn't work with me anymore, remember? Besides, I'm not proposing an orgy, just a quiet talk."

She glared at him. "Not in your room."

His grip lessened and he shrugged. "Have it your way, we'll eat in the Lodge dining room in full view of all the other diners. Is that public enough for you?"

He helped her step into the low-slung sports car and shut the door.

They did not dine in full view of the rest of the diners as he had promised, but at a secluded table partially hidden by lush hanging begonias in shades of scarlet and yellow and salmon. The glass wall behind them enhanced the garden setting with a view of the forest in which the Lodge was nestled.

Peter ordered Scotch on the rocks for both of them and Gina didn't object although she seldom drank whiskey. Maybe the smooth power of the amber liquid would give her the strength she needed to get through this discussion. She fingered the moist crystal glass as she said, "All right, Peter, I've waited all day for the other shoe to drop. What's this nonsense about us still being married?"

He took a hefty swallow of his drink and set it down. "It's not nonsense, I never filed for an annulment. If you didn't, and I know you didn't because I would have been notified, then you're still my wife."

Gina's aching head swam with confusion. "But I signed the papers! Your lawyer said that was all you wanted from me. He said after that I'd be free, and not to try to get any money from you because I wouldn't stand a snowball's chance in Hades of collecting."

Peter swore and actually sounded regretful as he said, "Sorry. I wasn't thinking rationally at the time. I fully expected to have to battle you in court over a settlement, though. The last thing I imagined was that you would run away, drop off the face of the earth."

He picked up the whiskey glass and drained it in one gulp. "Why, Ginny Lea? If you didn't want money, why did you marry me?"

There was a note of pleading in his voice, almost as if it was really important to him to know the truth. But she'd told him the truth, over and over and over, and she wasn't going to sink into that quagmire again. She took another sip of her drink before she answered. "We've been all through that, Peter, and my answer still stands. I loved you, and I thought you loved me. I never had sex with Mel or any other man, and I'm through defending myself to you. Now are we going to talk about the annulment or are you going to take me home?"

Before Peter could answer the waiter arrived with the oversized menus. Gina hadn't eaten all day; the thought of food made her ill and the sight of the menu with its dozen or so entries was depressing. Maybe a cup of broth and some crackers. Peter took the decision out of her hands by ordering for both of them. Split pea soup, tossed salad with the house dressing, stuffed salmon, baked potato with sour cream, and a bottle of Chardonnay. She protested that she couldn't possibly eat all that but neither Peter nor the waiter paid any heed.

When they were alone again he turned his full attention back to her. His blue eyes moved slowly over her taut face and rested on her slightly parted lips. "I told you, there was no annulment. If you don't believe me you can have your attorney check."

Gina shifted uneasily under his gaze. "I intend to. How could you marry Veronica if you were still married to me?"

His eyes narrowed. "I couldn't, and I didn't. I spent a lot of time in Europe and so did Veronica, and once in a while we'd run into each other. We were both staying at the same ski resort in Switzerland at the time of her accident."

He winced slightly, acknowledging a painful memory, then continued. "She went down the slope too fast and lost her balance on a curve. It—it was a long way down the side of that mountain."

Gina shivered as her mind portrayed the horror of the situation, and Peter paused thoughtfully. "It was up to me to notify her parents and make the arrangements to send her home. I don't know how the rumor got started that we were married. We didn't even travel together."

Gina was appalled at the feeling of relief that swept over her, relief that Peter had never married anyone else. Why should she care? He was nothing to her anymore. Nothing, that is, but an obstacle to her own marriage plans. How on earth was she going to tell Stewart?

The waiter arrived with bowls of thick steaming soup, and when he left Peter picked up the conversation as though he had been reading her mind. "Have you told Stewart yet?"

She jumped guiltily. "Told him what?" she asked evasively.

"That you can't marry him because you're married to me."

Gina choked on her soup. "Not for long I'm not. Are you going to file for annulment or shall I?"

Peter looked grim. "No."

She raised her eyebrows questioningly. "No what?"

"No, I'm not going to file for annulment and neither are you."

She dropped her empty spoon on the table. What new form of anguish had he devised for her now?

She glared at him. "Don't count on it! I'll contact a lawyer tomorrow."

He shook his head. "It won't do you any good."

"And just what is that supposed to mean?" she snapped.

He nonchalantly finished his last spoonful of soup before he replied. "If you petition for an annulment I'll swear that the marriage was consummated."

The shock that tore through Gina left her mute, which she realized later was just as well. If she'd opened her mouth she'd probably have screamed with pure frustration.

Who was this man who was tormenting her? He wasn't the gentle loving Peter Van Housen who had courted her with such tenderness and passion. Neither was he the agonized bridegroom striking out at her in his shock and pain. This man was cold and cruel and deliberately toying with her battered emotions. What's more, he was enjoying it!

She was vaguely aware that the waiter had appeared with their salads, and while he was clearing away the soup bowls and replacing them with the iced plates, the wine steward arrived with their wine. By the time the ceremony of tasting and approving and pouring had been completed, she had managed to pull her scattered thoughts together and find her voice.

"I think you must be out of your mind," she said gratingly.

"That's very possible," he agreed quite seriously. "After what you did to me, what you've put me through, it's surprising if I've retained any sanity at all, but I find that I like being married to an absentee wife. It doesn't hamper my—uh—movements in any way. And it's a sure-fire insurance policy against another ill-advised wedding. This way I can have my cake and eat it too, if you'll pardon the old cliché."

Gina slumped against the high-backed chair, defeated. Peter was a stranger, a vengeful stranger, and she didn't know how to handle him.

The pain in her head had become a pounding agony, and with a little moan she closed her eyes and lifted her cold glass to press it against her temples. Peter's large hand covered hers where it lay on the table and there was concern in his voice as he asked, "Ginny, what's wrong? Does your head hurt?"

She didn't want him to touch her, but she didn't seem to have the strength to pull away. "Yes, it does," she muttered. "I think you'd better take me home."

His hand closed around hers and squeezed it gently. "How long has it been since you've eaten?" he asked softly.

"I don't know, yesterday, last night I guess."

"Then it's no wonder you don't feel well. You shouldn't miss meals like that. Finish your whiskey and then start on your salad. There's no hurry, we've got all evening."

He picked up her hand and rubbed the back of it against his smooth, freshly shaven cheek. It sent a small shiver down her back. She opened her eyes and thought she saw regret written on his tanned face as he said, "It's all right, Ginny Lea, I promise we won't talk about anything unpleasant again tonight. Just relax and enjoy your dinner."

She did enjoy her dinner, and as the tension diminished so did her headache until it disappeared altogether. Peter skillfully changed the course of the conversation by talking about the new art gallery his father had built and about his own involvement in it. He explained that he would no longer be spending so much time abroad since they had recently hired a buyer who was tops in the field, and Peter would be taking over the family investment company when his father retired in the fall.

As the meal progressed and Peter kept her wine glass filled the subject changed from him to her and she found herself telling him about her college years, and her progress from a recent graduate to selling artist to gallery owner. It was all very friendly and informative, like two old friends getting together after an absence of seven years.

She noticed that he still called her Ginny Lea and asked him to use the more adult-sounding Gina instead. She couldn't bear to be reminded of how terribly young, vulnerable and in love Ginny Lea Brown had been. It wasn't until late in the evening as they lingered over dessert and coffee that she made the blunder—she mentioned her engagement to Stewart Tobias.

She felt Peter stiffen and his eyes, which had been alive with interest, narrowed and became noncommunicative. "Are you in love with Stewart, Gina?" he asked coldly.

"Of—of course," she answered, shaken by his unexpected query. "I wouldn't have agreed to marry him if I wasn't."

He threw his napkin on the table and signaled the waiter for the bill. "You agreed to marry me and all the time you were sleeping with Mel Calicutt," he accused.

The sudden attack was so unexpected that she was left temporarily off-balance and for a moment could only stare. Her breath caught in her throat as she said, "That's right, Peter. Go ahead and cling to those vicious misconceptions you've nourished so carefully all these years, but give me my freedom so I can marry the man who loves and trusts me."

Before he could reply the waiter approached and while Peter paid for the meal Gina regained her bearing and silently prepared to leave.

She should have known from the way he was behaving earlier that he would never let up. He had deliberately lured her into letting her guard down so that his next thrust would be all the more painful. He was determined to make her pay for her supposed sins, and if she wasn't careful he just might destroy her in the process.

They didn't speak on the way back to Gina's place, but Peter insisted on escorting her up the rickety outside stairway to her second-floor apartment. He took her key and unlocked her door then turned and in a surprise movement took her in his arms and kissed her. "Don't hate me, Gina," he pleaded thickly.

Before she could react he released her and bounded down the stairs to his car.

Gina had expected to toss and turn all night but instead her head had hardly settled into the pillow before she was asleep, and she woke feeling rested if not exactly enthusiastic about facing the day. It was foggy, and the gloomy weather matched her apprehensive mood.

Today she would have to talk to Stewart!

Stewart had kissed her good-bye after bringing her home from the wedding on Sunday and warned her that he was going to hole up in his mountain home for at least a week and try to catch up on the writing time he'd lost due to the festivities connected with the marriage of his daughter. Stewart frequently did this when he was working on a novel, and Gina knew that he would not contact her again until his spurt of inspiration ran dry. She accepted it as the price she paid for being engaged to a successful author with slightly unorthodox work habits.

After plugging in the coffee maker she phoned her part-time assistant, Peg Harvey, and asked her to open up the gallery this morning. She explained that she was going out of town and wouldn't be back until after lunch. After a quick breakfast she dressed in blue jeans, a short-sleeved light blue knit shirt and a navy long-sleeved sweat shirt. It was chilly in the Mendocino fog, but the sun would probably be shining at Stewart's hideaway.

It was only twenty minutes after seven o'clock when she headed her aging Datsun 220 north on Highway 1. Just outside of Fort Bragg she turned east on 20 and immediately started the climb into the heavily forested coastal mountain range. Within a few minutes the heavy fog began to lift and by the time she turned off onto the logging road that wound through the dense stands of sequoia sempervirens, the redwoods that stretched along the California coast from Big Sur to Oregon, she had rolled down her windows and was enjoying the warm sunshine. Gina loved the giant trees with their reddish bark and slender branches with leaves like those of a pine. An undergrowth of fern, vines and low bushes covered the ground and added a mustiness to the tangy odor of pine and cedar.

It wasn't yet eight o'clock when she spotted Stewart's small brown frame house set well back from the road and nearly hidden from view by California Black Oak and Pacific Dogwood trees. She turned the compact car into the long driveway and parked it beside the rose garden that was blooming profusely in every shade of red, white, yellow and pink. Her thick-soled shoes crunched across the gravel, and the four wooden stairs squeaked as she climbed to the covered porch that ran the full length of the front of the house. She didn't bother to knock but opened the unlocked front door and walked into the cluttered living room.

Gina heard the tap, tap, tap of Stewart's ancient typewriter and knew he was working in his office. She smiled to herself as she headed down the hall. It was a mystery to her why a man as intelligent as Stewart Tobias would resist all pleas to invest in a time- and labor-saving word processor. Instead he clung stubbornly to the twenty-year-old manual office model typewriter he had bought with the first paycheck he received for a writing assignment.

She stood unobserved in the open doorway and watched the large bearded man in faded jeans and a dirty white T-shirt who sat at the desk piled high with papers and books. His fingers ran expertly over the battered machine, and the deep creases on his wide brow gave mute evidence of complete concentration. Her heart seemed to turn over as she wondered how she was going to say what she had come to tell him. Would he be hurt? angry? disgusted with her for not telling him before of her early marriage? He had been so patient with her, but even Stewart's patience must have a breaking point.

He stopped typing but still he didn't notice her as he rummaged through the papers on his desk, obviously looking for something. Gina took a deep breath and spoke. "Hello darling."

He looked up, startled, and for a long moment he didn't seem to know who she was or how she got there. Then recognition dawned in his hazel eyes. "Gina!" he gasped and rose from his chair. "What are you doing here?"

They met in the middle of the room and embraced, but Stewart's kiss had an absent quality about it. It was the kiss of an author interrupted at his work who hasn't quite made it back to the real world yet. He glanced a little regretfully at his desk before he said, "Come in the kitchen, honey, and I'll pour us some coffee." He looked at his watch. "It's early, have you had breakfast?"

The kitchen was a disaster. Dirty dishes, empty beer cans, and the remains of the previous night's T.V. dinner littered the room. Stewart grinned sheepishly as he opened the window. "Sorry about the mess but I wasn't expecting company and I hated to take the time to clean it up."

Gina took two clean mugs from the cupboard and poured hot coffee from the electric percolator she had given him for his birthday last year after he'd "treated" her to a cup of boiled coffee warmed over for the umpteenth time. Ugh! Yes, Stewart definitely needed a wife, but did he want her badly enough to wait until she freed herself from Peter Van Housen? *And did she really want him to wait?*

That shocking and unbidden thought caused her hand to jerk and she spilled the brown liquid on the already stained tile countertop. Good heavens, what was the matter with her? Of course she wanted to marry Stewart. She loved him!

She mopped up the spill with a soggy dish cloth and handed one of the mugs to Stewart as she said, "Do you mind if we go into the living room? I think we'd be more—uh—comfortable."

Stewart frowned as he walked beside her. "I'm afraid it's not in much better shape. I really wish you'd phoned before you came, sweetheart. When I'm writing neither the house nor I are fit to be seen by anybody."

He led Gina to the brown leather sofa and cleared several magazines, books and a dirty sweat shirt off it before motioning her to sit down. He lowered himself beside her, careful not to spill his coffee, and she turned to him, at once eager and reluctant to explain.

"I'm sorry, Stewart," she began. "I know you don't like to be interrupted when you're working and ordinarily I wouldn't dream of just walking in on you this way, but I—I had to see you. I couldn't wait."

A grin lit Stewart's craggy face. "If I thought you meant that, my darling, I'd gladly chuck the manuscript and spend the day making love to you."

Gina felt her face grow hot with embarrassment and

she groaned inwardly. How could she have been so clumsy as to let him think even for a minute that . . . ?

"I—I didn't mean that," she stammered and realized she'd compounded her blunder as a shadow of pain flittered across his features before he could bring it under control.

"No," he murmured sadly, "I didn't think you did."

She wrapped her hands around the warm mug and took a deep breath. "I have something to tell you. I know now that I should have told you months ago, but I had no idea there would be so many—so many ramifications."

Stewart looked at her questioningly and she knew that the only way to start was at the beginning. "When I was eighteen I married Peter Van Housen," she blurted.

Stewart blanched. "You what?"

She took a swallow of her coffee and set it on the coffee table. "I was very young and naïve and I believed him when he said he loved me, but that was a long time ago. It won't make any difference to us. I hate him. He's a cruel, arrogant, son of a—"

Her voice had risen and she knew she sounded a little hysterical but she couldn't seem to control it. It was Stewart's hands cupping her shoulders and his cool voice that calmed her. "Take it easy, honey. Just take a deep breath and tell me what happened."

She did, and as the words poured out her thoughts seemed to pull together and she told the story much as she had told it to Twyla. She watched Stewart, wanting to gauge the hurt she was inflicting so she could ease it as much as possible. But his expression was closed, impersonal, and she had no idea what he was thinking or feeling.

Almost an hour later she brought her narration to a close by recounting Peter's abandonment and Mel's confession that he had arranged for the photograph and then given it to Veronica who in turn sent it to Peter. Stewart had been sitting quietly and, except for a muttered oath now and then, had made no comment. Now as she sat with her head bowed mutely looking at her hands twisted together in her lap, he reached for her and she snuggled into the safe protection of his embrace.

As she rested against his chest she could feel the tension that ran through him and she knew he wasn't as calm and collected as he wanted her to think. "You're right, Gina," he said. "You should have told me before. Now I understand why you've been so reluctant to let any man close to you, why you were in such a state at the wedding and reception."

His arms tightened around her. "I'll take care of Peter Van Housen," he muttered grimly. "When I get through with him he won't hurt you or bother you ever again. I guarantee it."

Gina wished she could just relax and let Stewart handle the matter, but she knew that was impossible. She hadn't finished her story, the most important point was yet to come. She disengaged herself from him and stood. "You don't understand, Stewart. Peter came to see me yesterday."

She started to walk restlessly away from the couch, then turned and looked back at him and clenched her fists as she continued, "He says that he never filed those annulment papers. He says we're still married. That I'm still his wife!"

Chapter Five

Gina watched the blood drain from his face as he stared at her, a look of shocked disbelief etched in his features. "Why would he keep the marriage intact all these years when it was *he* who walked out on *you?*" Stewart roared.

Gina shook her head. "I don't know, I was as stunned as you. He said something about an absentee wife giving him protection from making the same mistake again."

Stewart rose from the couch and swore with an earthiness Gina had never heard him use before. "Good Lord, you could have married and had children without ever knowing . . ."

His large frame filled the small room as he started to pace. "Well that's an oversight we can take care of in a hurry. Give me a couple of minutes to shower and change and I'll drive you to Fort Bragg. I know a lawyer there, she can get started on the annulment immediately. I think it can be taken care of in a matter of days."

He turned and took a few steps toward the bathroom before Gina caught him by the arm and said,
"No, Stewart, that won't do any good. Peter—he—he
said if I filed for annulment he would swear the
marriage was consummated."

Stewart glared at her with an all-consuming rage.
"And was it?" he grated.

Gina winced. "Of course not. I told you what
happened. I never saw him again after he walked out
of Mel's apartment until Saturday night at the wedding reception."

Stewart's gaze searched her face for a few seconds,
then with a muffled groan he took her in his arms and
held her close. "I'm sorry, baby," he murmured
shakily. "It's just that I can't stand the thought of any
other man touching you, and to know that—that"—
the name he called Peter was obscene in any language
—"has the legal right is galling beyond reason."

The legal right. The words struck terror in Gina.
Peter had the legal right to make love to her only if
she agreed to it. But after that traumatizing scene in
her kitchen yesterday morning she knew that her
mind would never overrule her body if he came at her
like that again. She had to end this farce of a
marriage, and quickly!

She shuddered and burrowed closer into Stewart's
arms. She wished now that she had married him
months ago when she had accepted his engagement
ring. It wouldn't have been legal, but maybe by this
time she would have been so passionately involved
with him that Peter could have had no emotional hold
over her.

Maybe, but she doubted it!

For several minutes she enjoyed the warm security

of Stewart's firm hard body, but then she sighed and pulled back to look at him. "Since Peter won't consent to an annulment I want a divorce," she said.

Stewart nodded. "That will take longer, but apparently it's the only solution. We'll drive down to San Francisco and see my lawyers about handling it. They'll put it through as quickly as possible."

It was Friday before she heard from Peter again.

It had been a busy day, profitable too. She'd not only sold two paintings by local artists, but an art teacher from San Jose had bought Gina's own seascape, a view of wind-swept waves, white and foamy, crashing against the rocks below the bluffs on which Mendocino was built. It had been priced higher than her others and she was pleased that he had paid the full price without wanting to bargain.

She was in the storage room at the back of the shop trying to select three pictures to replace the ones that had been purchased when she heard footsteps on the uncarpeted hardwood floors. She had her back to the door contemplating several paintings she had set up when the approaching footsteps stopped and she realized that someone was standing behind her. She looked over her shoulder and her heart jumped when she saw the blond, blue-eyed man dressed in a conservative gray business suit who looked like he was strongly tempted to throttle her. She spun around and was face to face with the thunderous countenance of Peter Van Housen.

She backed away and gasped, "What are you doing here?"

He grasped her shoulders roughly and his fingers bit into her tender flesh. "I can't turn my back on you for a minute can I?" he muttered furiously.

"I—I don't know what you're talking about," she stammered.

"No?" he hissed savagely. "Then I'll show you."

With a suddenness that took her totally off guard he pulled her against him and kissed her, an angry, brutal kiss that ground the inside of her mouth against her teeth and bruised her lips. She struggled but he held her in a tight grasp that left her no room to maneuver and she was helpless to defend herself. Her air supply was nearly cut off and the more she twisted the harder it was to breathe. She felt dizzy and in an automatic bid for survival she stopped struggling and relaxed.

Once she was no longer fighting, Peter's mouth on hers gentled and his grip on her eased. Before she could attempt to break away from him one of his hands began a languorous trail down her spine while the other one gently caressed her shoulders. She shivered as unbidden sensations surged through her and her arms, no longer imprisoned at her sides, crept around his waist.

His lips ceased punishing, but now explored her face with exquisite tenderness. Her eyes, her cheeks, the corners of her mouth. His white even teeth nibbled delicately at her ear lobes and her arms tightened around him as her fingers splayed over the rippling muscles of his back.

He nuzzled the sensitive hollow at the side of her neck, and the sensations became pinpricks of fire that set her squirming against him in an effort to placate the smoldering desire that had robbed her of all reason. Her seductive movements elicited a moan of passion from Peter and his mouth again sought hers with a tender but urgent craving.

A voice calling her name finally penetrated Gina's

consciousness and with it her sanity returned. She pushed away from Peter, horrified by her total surrender, but he didn't release her immediately. Instead he held her by the arms and there was a look of triumph on his face as his gaze slid over her swollen lips and her wide violet eyes, still clouded with passion.

"Now tell me you want to divorce me and marry Stewart Tobias," he said in a voice tinged with amusement.

Gina was too enraged to speak, and before she could hurl all the epithets that were gathering in her mind, the Junoesque figure of Twyla Sisson appeared in the doorway. "Oh, Gina, there you are," she said. "I've been looking—"

She closed her mouth abruptly when she saw Peter and her quick searching look must have correctly assessed the situation because she started to back away. "Oh, sorry."

Gina sprang to life. "No, Twyla, please don't leave!"

Twyla must have picked up the tone of desperation in Gina's voice because she hesitated as Gina continued, "Have—have you met Peter Van Housen? Peter, this is my friend, Twyla Sisson. She owns the—"

"I've met Twyla," Peter interrupted rudely, "but it was quite some time ago. How are you, Twyla?"

Twyla nodded in acknowledgment but she didn't answer his question. Instead her expressive brown eyes watched him narrowly as she said, "So you're the husband?"

Peter nodded curtly. "I see you've been brought up to date on the state of my relationship with Gina."

That was true. On Wednesday, the day after Stewart and Gina had driven to San Francisco where Gina filed suit for dissolution of marriage from Peter, she had gone to see Twyla and once again unburdened her problems and fears on her friend. Twyla had listened and comforted her, and had done Gina the honor of not giving unsolicited and useless advice. Instead she had supplied a shaker of dry martinis and offered to loan her money if she needed it for legal fees.

Twyla didn't bat an eyelash as she replied to Peter's observation. "Yes I have, does that make you uncomfortable?"

Peter's mouth quirked in a humorless smile. "Not at all, *I* have nothing to be uncomfortable about. I do want to talk to Gina, however, so if you'll excuse us we'll go up to her apartment where we can have a little privacy."

His hand cupped Gina's elbow but she pulled away from him. "No!" she cried, louder than she had intended. She lowered her voice and turned to Twyla, her features twisted with anxiety. "Come with us, Twyla. Please!"

The pleading tone couldn't be missed, and Twyla put her arm around Gina's slender shoulders and started to walk with her toward the front of the gallery. "Of course I'll come if you want me to." She chuckled. "Frankly, I wouldn't miss it."

Upstairs in Gina's apartment she and Twyla sat on the sofa and Peter sat in a chair across from them. Gina perched stiffly on the edge of the couch, her hand gripping the arm as she said, "All right, Peter, you said you wanted to talk to me so please, let's get it over with."

Peter frowned as he glanced at Twyla, then apparently decided to ignore her as he turned back to look at Gina. "I arrived at my office a little late this morning and found a man there waiting to serve me with divorce papers," he said angrily. "I told you I'd fight an annulment."

"I didn't file for annulment," she answered grimly. "I filed for dissolution."

His eyes were as cold as blue ice. "Did you really think I'd give you a divorce after I'd refused to consent to an annulment?"

The swift jab of his words landed in the pit of her stomach, and she gasped and bent forward slightly as though to protect herself from another attack. "You swine!" she hissed through clenched teeth. "Why are you doing this? What do you want of me?"

Peter lounged back in his chair, and the only sign that he was not totally relaxed was the deepening lines of strain around his mouth and the pulse that throbbed at his temple. "I want the same thing any man wants from his wife—a companion, a lover, a mother for my children."

Gina jumped to her feet and stared at him. "You're out of your mind!" she screamed. "Seven years ago you told me you wouldn't touch me if I were the only woman on earth and then, despite my pleadings, you walked out on me and I didn't see you again until five days ago. Now you refuse to terminate the marriage. Why? Surely you're not going to try to tell me you love me!"

Peter rose suddenly as though jerked from the chair and walked away from her. "Love!" he spat out, as though it were a dirty word. "No, I'm not telling you I love you. You cured me of that adolescent affliction with one well-placed thrust years ago. But I find that I'm still physically attracted to you, as you are to me."

She drew in her breath sharply and he whirled around to face her. "Oh, don't bother to deny it," he jeered. "Twice now we have come together and nearly gone up in smoke, both of us, together. You were just as aroused as I so don't stand there sputtering."

Gina knew it was true, and her innate sense of honesty would not allow her to deny it. Instead she turned away from him as he continued to talk. "I'm thirty-three years old and bored with my life style. I want to settle down with a wife and start a family, and since I'm already married to you I see no reason to delay. You're beautiful, talented, well-educated and sexually exciting, everything I want in a wife."

Gina was too stunned to protest. Peter didn't love her, and he knew she didn't love him, but still he wanted to live with her as husband and wife. He wanted her to be his housekeeper, his hostess, his convenient sex partner. He even wanted her to bring children into that cold, sterile environment! The man was insane! Surely he didn't really believe that she could live like that.

She straightened her shoulders and turned to look at him. "I'm surprised at you, Peter," she said as she strove to sound calm and a little disdainful. "Are you forgetting the reason why our marriage never got started? The picture? My so-called promiscuity? As I remember you called me a wh—"

"Stop it Gina!" he snapped before she could finish the coarse word. "I'm not forgetting, I only wish I could, but you had forced me into marriage on the premise that you were a virgin and too pure to make love with me until it was legal. When I saw that picture and realized that all you wanted was my money and social position I went a little mad."

His hands clutched the back of the chair he had been sitting in and she could see the muscles flex in his arms. "I'm older now," he continued, "and more tolerant of your sexual experience."

She cringed at the coldness of his words, and her only thought was to hurt him as he had hurt her. "But aren't you afraid I might revert to my old ways and take lovers on the side?" she taunted.

She thought she saw him wince, but if so he checked it quickly and forced a grin that was more of a grimace. "The thought never occurred to me. I intend to keep you too—well satisfied—to have the urge or the energy for anybody but me."

Something inside Gina seemed to shrivel and her shoulders slumped. She should have known better than to play word games with Peter Van Housen; no one ever bested him in anything. She rubbed her temples with her fingers as she said, "You forget, I'm in love with Stewart. I'm going to marry him just as soon as our lawyers can bring this dissolution action to court so don't make any long-range plans about playing house with me. I'll see you in hell first."

She didn't hear him move on the carpeted floor, and she jumped as his hands gripped her shoulders and pulled her back against the long length of him. She could feel his warm breath on her cheek. "Then you'd better dress in something cool because you'll be there a long time," he murmured softly. "I have a team of the best attorneys in the west and they have a lot of political clout. We can and will delay this dissolution hearing indefinitely."

His fingers tightened to a bruising hold and his voice hardened. "Meanwhile stay out of Stewart Tobias's bed. I won't have my wife sleeping with another man."

He released her suddenly and walked out of the apartment slamming the door behind him.

Several days later a letter arrived from her attorney stating that Mr. Van Housen had declared his intention to contest the suit for dissolution and therefore the proceedings would be more complicated than first thought. Gina crumpled the heavy bond paper in her hand and knew that she could no longer put off telling Stewart about this latest impediment to gaining her freedom. She couldn't take the chance that Peter might contact him directly. He and Stewart had apparently been friends until she entered the picture but now they hated each other's guts.

She gazed at the cream-colored telephone on her desk. There was no need for her to drive all the way back up to the cabin when she could call and talk to him. He was busy and so was she; there was no need to waste a whole day on this. After all it was just a matter of keeping him informed; it wasn't something they had to talk at length about.

She picked up the phone and her hand hovered over the dial. What was she going to say to him? *We'll have to postpone the wedding indefinitely, darling, my husband won't give me a divorce?* Or maybe, *My husband is holding up the divorce, dear, but I know you won't mind remaining celibate for two or three more years until you can legally go to bed with me."*

Gina slammed the phone back in its cradle with a resounding bang and dropped her heated face in her hands. Damn! Why did everything have to be so complicated? Couldn't she just once have simple problems like other people? Was there no end to this nightmare?

She loved Stewart. He was kind and considerate and he loved her deeply, and still it was Peter who aroused her to a fever pitch. This situation couldn't go on and it was time she did something about it.

Again she reached for the phone and dialed quickly. Stewart answered on the first ring. "Gina," he exclaimed happily, "I was just thinking about you."

"I was thinking about you, too," Gina said, "and I—Stewart, I want to see you."

"Not as much as I want to see you, sweetheart," he answered huskily. "How about tomorrow evening? I have some business to take care of in Fort Bragg and I have to shop for supplies, I'm running out of everything up here. I'll pick you up about six and we'll have dinner, okay? I've missed you like crazy."

She realized that he'd put the wrong interpretation on her request to see him but it was too late now. She'd try to explain tomorrow without hurting him.

Gina made a special effort to sound happy and enthusiastic as she agreed. They talked for a few minutes and just before he rang off he said, "I love you, Gina."

The words, meant to reassure, made her feel like the cheat Peter thought she was. What a tragic mess, she thought as she replaced the phone. Stewart loved her and she loved Peter.

"Oh no!" she groaned aloud as she brought her pondering thoughts to a screeching halt. She couldn't love Peter! She couldn't be so stupid as to fall in love with Peter Van Housen all over again. She'd had enough of loving that man to last her a lifetime. She was not a masochist, she was an intelligent, well-educated woman who had risen from the rubble of a shattered romance once and had no intention of repeating the performance. She wasn't going to revert back to the lovesick little ninny who didn't know the difference between a man's love and his lust.

So, fine, she would somehow keep her desire for

Peter under control, but what about Stewart? Could she in all decency remain engaged to him when her body cried out for another man? That was the basest type of dishonesty, but wasn't it better than telling him the truth? Stewart loved her enough to wait for her and she'd be a good wife to him. Surely she was woman enough to simulate a passion she didn't feel. He need never know—

Don't be such a self-deceiving hypocrite! she mentally castigated herself. Of course Stewart would know. He was a loving and sensitive man and she would hurt him far more by marrying him than she would by making a clean break of it now. She would never live with Peter as his wife, but neither could she offer Stewart second-best. When she saw him tomorrow she would give him back his ring.

That proved to be easier said than done. She decided not to have dinner with him but to tell him as soon as he arrived and not prolong the agony. Still she didn't want to greet him looking tired and grubby after a day's work, so she left the gallery early and went upstairs to shower and change into a mint green dress with a large ruffle at the low V-neckline that widened to a short cape at the shoulders and back. She added a touch of matching green eye shadow to accent her violet eyes, and a cherry shade of lip gloss completed her make-up.

When Stewart arrived he swept her into his arms and planted a long, lingering kiss on her soft willing mouth. She couldn't hurt him by resisting, and besides she liked to have him kiss her. He didn't arouse her to a smoldering passion, but his kisses represented warmth, stability and security. She could have been happy married to this loving older man if Peter hadn't come into her life again.

He held her close and his beard felt soft against her cheek. "I've missed you, darling," he murmured. "Let's get married before I start my next book. I want you with me, even though I'm not very good company when I'm writing."

Gina cringed inside at the thought of what she must do, but it couldn't be put off. Now was the time. Stewart had brought up the subject of marriage and had given her the perfect opening.

She took a quick breath and began. "Stewart, I—"

He hugged her hard and then released her. "I know, baby, I promised I wouldn't rush you into marriage. I *am* going to hurry you about eating though. I'm starved. We have reservations for seven o'clock at the Steak & Lobster and it's at least a half-hour drive up that winding coast highway, so get a move on."

He laughed and Gina ducked into the bedroom to pick up her shawl. He was in a good mood. The least she could do was let him enjoy his dinner before she clobbered him.

The restaurant was situated on a bluff overlooking the ocean, and both the food and the scenery were outstanding. They ordered lobster and were given huge bibs that tied around their necks to protect their clothes when they dipped the succulent white chunks of meat into small pots of warm melted butter that often dripped as they raised it to their mouths.

As though by mutual consent they kept the conversation light. Stewart talked about the letter he'd received from his honeymooning daughter and Gina told him of the highly profitable two weeks she'd had at the gallery. Later they danced to the music of the four-piece combo and he told her how beautiful she was and how much he wanted to make her his own. It was then that she asked him to take her home.

It was about eleven o'clock when they arrived back at her apartment and Gina poured them each double portions of Scotch over ice. Stewart raised one speculative eyebrow and grinned. "What are you trying to do, sweetheart, get us both bombed? After all that wine with dinner and now this I may wind up sleeping on your couch tonight. That is unless you'd rather I shared your bed."

Gina sat down at the other end of the couch from him. "I have to talk to you, Stewart," she said.

He chuckled. "About sharing your bed? If you ask me nicely I think I could be persuaded." He held out his hand to her. "What are you doing way over there? Come here and let me show you what a nice bed partner I could be."

She moved to sit closer to him, but when he tried to take her in his arms she resisted. "Please, Stewart, I'm serious."

His teasing tone immediately vanished and he looked at her with a wariness he made no attempt to hide. "I'm sorry, Gina," he said quietly. "I didn't realize. Tell me about it."

Before she could lose her nerve Gina removed the stunning diamond ring from the third finger of her left hand and looked at it as she held it in her palm. "I'm returning your ring. I—I can't marry you. I'm sorry."

She had expected arguments, recriminations, almost anything but the total silence that followed. Finally, when the quiet seemed to close in on her, she raised her head and looked at him. There was a veiled expression in his eyes and she knew he had successfully masked whatever emotion he might have been feeling.

He watched her for a moment then said, "It's Peter Van Housen, isn't it?"

She looked away again. "I—I'm married to him and he's contesting the divorce. He told me yesterday. It may be a long time until I'm free."

"By free do you mean you're going ahead with the dissolution?" He sounded like a disinterested bystander.

"Of course, but he intends to fight it every step of the way. He has a lot of money, he can hire the best lawyers and it may be months, years even, before I can get a hearing."

Stewart took a gulp of his whiskey. "I have a lot of money too, and I'm not without influence. I can hire lawyers who are just as smart as his, and I will if you're truly serious about wanting out of the marriage."

She gripped the ring in her fist. "I can't let you do that."

Again there was silence, broken at last by Stewart's voice, tender this time. "Look at me, Gina." She lifted her gaze to his and he asked, "Are you still in love with him?"

She dampened her lips with the tip of her tongue in an unconsciously appealing gesture. "I don't know," she answered truthfully. "I don't want to be. He doesn't love me, he told me so. He let me down badly when I desperately needed his love and trust. It would be sheer folly for me to fall in love with him again. Even so I can't help responding to him."

She saw it then, the sharp stab of agony that flicked across his face and made him cringe. Without thinking she uttered a little cry of compassion and moved into his arms.

He held her close and she buried her face in the curve between his shoulder and throat. "Oh, Stewart," she moaned softly. "I'm so sorry. I didn't want to hurt you this way. I really do love you, you know."

For a few minutes he just held her and didn't try to talk, but finally, when he did speak his voice was under control. "I know how you feel about me, baby. I've never kidded myself that you loved me the way I love you. It would have been enough for me because I wanted you on any terms I could get you, but not if you're in love with another man."

The tears she'd been fighting to hold back brimmed over and spilled down her cheeks and onto his shirt as she sobbed. "I wish I'd met you first."

He rubbed his bearded cheek against her temple. "Even if you had it wouldn't have worked for us. Remember, I'm almost as old as your father. When you were eighteen I was in my middle thirties and had a wife and teenage daughter not much younger than you. You wouldn't have given me a second thought."

He fumbled in his back pocket and handed her a white linen handkerchief. "Don't cry for me, Gina," he said as he lifted her away from him. "Save your tears, you're going to need them for yourself if you let Peter Van Housen back in your life again."

He stood and put on his suit coat while Gina dried her eyes and blew her nose. She balled the handkerchief in her hand and got up feeling awkward and uneasy. How was she going to handle the good-byes?

Stewart did it for her. He dropped his hands on her shoulders and said, "You're welcome to keep the ring. I have no use for it."

It was only then that she remembered she still held

it and raised her closed fist palm up. She opened her fingers slowly and gazed at the glittering stone. "I'm sorry, I'd forgotten I still had it. Maybe that says something to both of us, Stewart. It's a sign that I find it hard to give you up, and for that reason I must not keep it. It—it has to be a final break, for both our sakes."

He took it from her and shoved it in his pocket. "Perhaps you're right." He put his arm around her waist and led her to the door.

He turned toward her then and put his other arm around her, holding her loosely against him. "Good luck, my darling."

His lips touched hers for just a moment and then he was gone.

Chapter Six

Shortly after lunch on Friday, as Gina sat at the desk in her cramped little office off the main room of the gallery trying to balance her checkbook, the phone rang. It was Peter. She'd have known his voice anywhere, and if her ear hadn't there were other parts of her anatomy that did, including her heart. It seemed to leap within her and then started pounding at an appalling speed.

Her thoughts went back seven years when she had experienced exactly the same reaction every time he'd telephoned her. She would wait impatiently for a call, then race to answer the phone when it rang and close her eyes, the better to savor every nuance of that incredibly sexy voice that sent a wave of pure ecstasy washing through her pulsating young body.

The wave was back again and she clenched the receiver like a lifeline to keep from being drowned in emotions she would not, dared not, experience again.

Peter must have misunderstood her silence because he rushed to fill it with words. "Please, Gina, don't hang up. What I have to say is important."

He sounded alarmed, as though he would go to any lengths to keep her on the other end of the line.

She pressed her hand to her fluttering stomach and answered. "I have no intentions of hanging up, but I am busy. I hope we can keep this conversation short."

"I'm sorry if I've caught you at a bad time," he apologized, "but I've promised my sister Lillian's two kids that I'd take them to Fort Bragg this weekend to ride the Skunk Train and we'd like for you to come with us."

"Lilly's children?" Gina was confused. "But they're just babies!"

Peter chuckled and some of the tension vanished from his tone. "Not anymore they're not. Sonja's eight and Johnny's ten and they're a handful. I need help in shepherding the two little brats. Come on, be a good sport and help me play nursemaid tomorrow."

Gina couldn't believe that the youngsters who had been a babe in arms and a toddler could have grown so fast. But then, it hadn't been fast at all. It had been seven long lonely, painful years since she'd last seen them on her wedding day. It was hard to believe that time hadn't stopped for everybody the way it had for her.

Fortunately she didn't have to make up an excuse, she had one that couldn't be disputed. "Peter, I can't go anywhere tomorrow, Saturday's one of our busiest days at the gallery."

"Surely you have employees," he observed.

"Yes, of course, I have an assistant, but Peg and I are both kept busy on the weekends."

Peter hesitated. "Sundays too?"

Gina was relieved to be able to tell him yes, Sundays too.

He began to sound annoyed. "You're not going to make me believe that you spend all your time in that shop. What days do you have off?"

Now she was caught. Oh darn, she should have known it wouldn't be easy to sidestep Peter Van Housen when he wanted something of her. She sighed and answered truthfully, "All day Monday and part of Tuesday, but I have housecleaning and laundry and—"

"Please, Gina," Peter interrupted, and the alarm was back in his voice. "Look, I'm sorry about the way our last meeting ended. I promise to be on my best behavior this time. With two kids as chaperones I won't be able to make such a jerk of myself as I usually do."

Gina was too astounded to reply. Was he actually apologizing to her? Admitting that he might be wrong? No, not Peter. Everyone else in the world might be wrong but never Peter. So why didn't she just tell him no and hang up?

His voice dropped to a husky murmur. "Gina, I want to see you. You know that I'm not so overflowing with paternal instinct that I routinely borrow my niece and nephew for a weekend of child-oriented fun and games. I want to spend a day with *you*, but I was afraid if I showed up alone you'd slam the door in my face."

His seductive tone and the words he was uttering were rapidly melting her resistance and she had to get control of the conversation before her overactive glands prodded her into ignoring her better judgment. "Peter—" she began tentatively.

"I'll bring the kids up Sunday night and we'll take the train ride Monday," he interrupted. "I swear we won't be alone together for a minute, we'll be too busy trying to keep track of those little monsters of Lil's."

In her mind Gina pictured Peter and herself each clutching the hand of a small child—daddy, mommy and the children. The family they could so easily have been by now. She shut her eyes trying to block out the image but it only seemed to bring Peter closer as his soft words sounded intimately in her ear. "I need to spend some time with you, darling. It's been so long, so very long."

Gina felt tears rising in her throat and when she spoke her words came out on a choked sob. "Oh Peter, don't. Please don't. I won't—I can't—let you hurt me anymore."

There was a catch in Peter's voice too as he said, "I don't want to hurt you, Gina, I want to make love to you. I won't, though, not until you want me as much as I want you."

He cleared his throat and his tone became more even. "We'll pick you up at seven-thirty Monday morning and take you out to breakfast. Don't keep us waiting because the train leaves from Fort Bragg at nine-twenty."

Gina hung up the phone without answering and dropped her head in her hands. Why didn't she tell him no? What was she letting herself in for?

The alarm went off early on Monday morning and Gina had just finished dressing in jeans and a blue bandana print sleeveless blouse when Peter arrived with a towheaded youngster in each hand. He introduced the taller one on the right as Johnny and the petite one on the left as Sonja. "This lovely lady's name is Virginia," he said to the children, "but I'm sure she won't mind if you call her Aunt Gina."

Gina's violet eyes widened, but Peter couldn't have looked more innocent and besides there wasn't anything else she could do but agree without being rude. "Yes, please do," she said as she shook hands with each child in turn.

Eight-year-old Sonja looked at Gina and asked, "Do you have a last name?"

Peter answered for her. "Indeed she does, it's—"

"Brown," interjected Gina hastily just in case he had intended to say Van Housen. Gina Van Housen. It sounded strange. She'd never thought of herself as Gina Van Housen and she wasn't going to start now.

"My full name is Virginia Lea Brown," she answered the little girl, "but my friends call me Gina. Now let me see, if I remember right your last name is Wilcox."

Sonja's freckled face brightened with surprise. "How did you know?" she squealed.

"I used to know your mother," answered Gina.

"But Mommie never told us about you."

I'll just bet she didn't, thought Gina as she picked up the red cardigan she'd laid out to wear. Lilly Wilcox had been just as opposed to Gina marrying Peter as his parents had been.

They had breakfast at a restaurant in Fort Bragg that catered to the tourist trade, fast, clean and edible. The Wilcox children were bright, lively and well-mannered, and Peter was on his best behavior. He indulged the youngsters when they insisted on ordering pancakes with syrup and hot fudge sundaes, and grinned at Gina when she allowed herself an exaggerated shudder. He kept the conversation light and strictly impersonal and she began to relax.

At the small railroad depot they picked up the tickets Peter had reserved by phone and took their place in line with the three-hundred-plus other passengers waiting to board one of the five red, gold and black cars with the funny black and white caricature of a skunk, appropriately wearing a conductor's cap, that was painted on the sides. Johnny was especially interested in the diesel-powered locomotive which pulled and pushed the coaches and observation car into position on the track while the crowd watched. He badgered his uncle with questions and Peter, reading from a booklet he'd bought, explained that the engine was built by the Baldwin Locomotive Works at its Eddystone, Pennsylvania plant in 1924 and weighed 234,600 pounds.

Finally the train was maneuvered into place and the passengers were allowed to board. Peter let Sonja and Johnny pick the coach they wanted and they chose the one named *Noyo*. Peter wanted to turn one of the bench seats so the four of them could sit facing each other, but both children wanted to sit by the window and neither of them would agree to sit backwards so Gina sat with Sonja and Peter and Johnny shared the seat ahead of them.

The conductor shouted a happy "All aboard?" and the train lurched into motion. They chugged slowly east through Fort Bragg, along colorful Pudding Creek and into the spectacular mountain country between Fort Bragg and Willits. Sonja's eyes sparkled with the excitement of a little girl on her first train ride. She kept up a constant stream of chatter that Gina quickly realized didn't demand an answer, so she leaned back in the seat and watched as the forest deepened.

It was promising to be a beautiful day. Not only the weather, which grew warmer with each mile they traveled, but the company. Peter's eyes had roamed

over her with undisguised admiration when she'd
opened her door for him that morning, and ever since
he'd been like the Peter she used to know, fun,
exciting and charming. He was at ease with his niece
and nephew, neither too strict nor too lenient—except
in the case of the pancakes and ice cream—and they
obviously adored him.

A pretty young tour guide wearing a black jumper
decorated with the black and white skunk logo and a
white blouse stood at the front of the car and with the
aid of a public address system welcomed them to the
world-famous California Western Railroad Super
Skunk Line. She explained that it was originated as a
logging railroad in 1885 and was powered by gas
engines which prompted folks to say, "You can smell
'em before you can see 'em." Thus the nickname.

Most of the passengers giggled but Sonja and
Johnny thought it was an hilarious joke and screamed
with laughter, prompting Peter and Gina to quiet
them so they could hear the guide explain that steam
passenger service was started in 1904 and extended to
Willits in 1911, thus connecting by rail the two towns
on either side of the Coastal Mountain Range.

After they had passed through the first of the two
tunnels on the line Sonja and Johnny wanted to join
some of the other passengers on the open observation
car, and Gina and Peter accompanied them. Peter
lifted Sonja in his arms so she could view the sleepy
Noyo river for which their car was named. They
snaked along the curved track in the shadows of
majestic, towering redwoods and over high trestles—
some wooden, some metal—that spanned the river
and the gulches.

After a while Sonja got restless in Peter's arms and
wanted to get down. The clear fresh mountain

breeze ruffled Gina's pixie haircut as Peter's hand gripped hers where it grasped the railing. She looked up and he frowned down at her. "Why aren't you wearing your ring?"

Now was not the time to tell him she'd broken off with Stewart, she'd need privacy for that. Instead she said, "The diamond was loose. I'm having it repaired."

Peter's gaze held hers as though he was trying to decide whether or not she was telling the truth. Finally he looked away and changed the subject. "Have you taken this trip before?"

She nodded. "Several times. Twyla took me shortly after I came here, and later I took Dad and Mama."

Peter watched a small deer bound through the trees. "How are your parents? Is your father still in the service?"

Her gaze followed his until the graceful fawn disappeared. "Yes, they're stationed in a rather remote part of Germany, have been for over a year. He hopes to stay there until he retires in three more years."

"Do you miss them, Gina?" he asked. "I remember that you and your mother were more like sisters than mother and daughter."

Gina smiled. "Mama was only eighteen when I was born. We sort of grew up together."

She was silent for a moment. "Yes," she continued, "I miss them. I'd like to see them more often, but Dad and Mama are still lovers, they don't need anybody but each other and I am completely self-sufficient."

Peter drew in his breath as his hand tightened on hers. "Are you so sure of that? You didn't used to be. As I remember you were more dependent than most eighteen-year-olds."

Gina winced as she remembered how totally she

had centered her young life on Peter Van Housen. How stupidly she had assumed he'd take care of her, cherish her forever.

She pulled her hand from under his and turned away. "I grew up fast after I left San Francisco," she said bitterly. "I never lived with my parents again. During my college years I roomed in a dormitory, and after I graduated I came out here. Oh yes, Peter, I can take care of myself all right."

Thanks to you, she almost added but stopped herself in time. She didn't want this conversation to go any further.

Peter gripped her shoulders and pulled her back against him. "Did you and Mel Calicutt quarrel?" he asked, his mouth close to her ear. "Is that the reason you stopped seeing him?"

Gina sighed. She'd never make him understand. He would never believe that she and Mel hadn't been lovers.

She jerked away from his grasp and turned to face him. "You'd better believe we quarreled!" she shouted over the noise of the train and the babble of voices. "After that outrageous lie he told you I called him every vile name I could think of and walked out. I heard later that he left town."

She tried to walk away but Peter caught her arm. "Why would he lie to me, Gina? What reason could he possibly have? He couldn't stop the wedding, we were already married."

She opened her mouth to say, *because your precious Veronica paid him to,* but then closed it again and choked back the words. What good would it do to tell him? He wouldn't believe her and Veronica was dead. It seemed distasteful to make accusations against a woman who couldn't fight back, especially when Gina couldn't produce any evidence of her own to back them up.

Instead she shrugged and muttered, "If I told you you wouldn't believe me."

Just then the train ground to a noisy halt at Northspur, a quiet area in a grove of redwoods where light refreshments were available from several stands and a beer garden. Some of the passengers were also changing trains here to return to Fort Bragg.

The children headed for the nearest food stand and Peter and Gina forgot their argument in the rush to keep track of them among the several hundred disembarking passengers. All four of them ordered hamburgers and colas and took them to a grassy spot in the shade where they sat cross-legged on the ground and ate with a relish that surprised Gina. She hadn't expected to be so hungry after her big breakfast. *It must be the fresh mountain air,* she decided.

Sonja and Johnny finished their sandwiches and begged for ice cream cones. Peter solemnly announced that if they weren't careful they would turn into a giant glob of ice cream, then gave them each a dollar and told them to "live it up." The children ran happily toward the nearest ice cream stand and he lay back on the grass with his hands under his head. Gina sat with her knees drawn up and her arms wrapped around her legs.

Peter reached over and clasped his hand around her nylon-clad ankle. "Lie down beside me, Gina," he commanded softly.

His touch sent a tremor up her leg and she had an unreasoning desire to do as he asked. To stretch out beside him in the privacy afforded by the huge tree trunk and surrounding bushes. She remembered the times they had lain together, on the beach, on the sofa, even in the car, while he'd made love to her. Slowly at first, only a touch, but building in passion until it took every ounce of will power she possessed to stop him before the final, irrevocable union of their trembling bodies.

She shivered and tried to move her foot but he wouldn't release it. Instead he renewed his request. "Curl up here on the grass and rest for a while."

"No," she said brusquely.

He rolled over on his side and propped his head up on his elbow. "Come here, Gina."

He let loose of her ankle and ran his fingers lightly along her bare arm. She had discarded her cardigan earlier, but now she wished she hadn't as his touch on her skin seemed to melt all of her resistance.

"I won't hurt you, I just want you near me," he pleaded in that soft, sexy tone, and she sank to the ground, mesmerized by blue eyes grown dark with yearning.

His finger traced the planes and hollows of her delicate, triangular-shaped face as he studied her changing expressions closely. The feathery strokes created a delicious tickling sensation against her creamy complexion, then changed direction to follow the line of her jaw.

"My beautiful, tantalizing wife," he murmured dreamily. "Most women lose that dewy freshness as the years go by, but you're even lovelier than you were at eighteen."

She knew she should stop him, but she couldn't seem to raise her hand to brush his away. Instead she protested half-heartedly, "I'm not your wife."

"Yes you are." His finger moved to the sensitive spot behind her ear. "The marriage hasn't been consummated but you're legally my wife and I want you. I want you almost as bad as I did the day we were married."

He picked up her right hand and placed it against his chest. "Here, feel."

She could feel the fast beat of his heart beneath the thin shirt he wore. She was also aware of the mat of dark blond hair that she had so often run her fingers through in the past. She'd always wondered why the hair on his chest was so much darker than the hair on his head, which in those days had been almost platinum.

Before she realized what he was doing he'd unbuttoned his shirt and moved her hand inside to rest against the warmth of his nude flesh. She tried to pull away but he kept his hand over hers until, with a mind of its own, it began to move caressingly through the tangle of hair. Immediately she felt his heartbeat speed up and he grinned down at her. "See what you do to me?" he whispered.

Her gaze locked with his and she gasped as she felt his hand on her left breast. His heartbeat was erratic now as was her own. He leaned over and nuzzled the sensitive spot at the side of her throat and she quivered with desire. At the same time his heart was turning somersaults under her touch.

He raised his head and put his mouth against her ear. "Your heart is pounding as hard as mine." His voice was thick with suppressed passion. "We strike sparks off each other, sweetheart, that light fires we can only quench together. Come live with me, Gina. It doesn't matter that we don't love each other, we'll get along great in bed and that's all that really counts in a marriage."

The strident sound of the train whistle rent the air and brought them both upright. They scrambled to

their feet and started searching for the children
among the crowd of people waiting to board the train
again to continue their journey across the mountains
to Willits.

She was devoutly thankful for that whistle. Without
it there was no telling what she might have agreed to!

As they started the second leg of their journey,
Gina curled up on her end of the bench seat and tried
to quiet her still racing heart. Why, oh why did she
allow Peter to arouse her so? Even as she asked the
question she knew she had no choice in the matter.
He'd always had that effect on her, and in spite of the
hell he'd put her through her body still responded to
him even though her brain told her to cool it. So much
for the power of intellect over emotion!

She was glad they weren't sitting together. She
needed time away from that openly sensuous gaze of
his to try to regroup her defenses. Why didn't he leave
her alone? He still thought she intended to marry
Stewart.

That was probably what motivated him, the prepos-
terous idea that she could want to belong to another
man. Peter didn't love her, but he wasn't about to let
any other man have her. Well, she'd show him. She
wasn't going to let the undeniable sexual attraction
she felt for him ruin her life again. No way!

After leaving Northspur the climb was rapid, seven
hundred and one feet in nine miles with horseshoe
curves as much as twenty-five degrees, according to
their pretty little tour guide. At one point they could
look down from the first car and see the last car far
below just starting to make the turn.

The children kept Gina and Peter occupied with
their persistent questions and chatter. Finally after
something over an hour the train reached the

one-thousand-seven-hundred-and-forty-foot summit, roared through another tunnel, and started the four-and-a-half-mile descent down the other side of the mountain range to Willets.

It was hot in the small city at the eastern end of the Skunk Line. At least twenty degrees hotter than it had been on the coast earlier that morning, but they had all dressed for the swift change of climate. Peter and the children, like Gina, had worn cool shirts under sweaters which they removed as the weather got warm. Some of the passengers had brought picnic lunches and headed for the nearby park, but Peter herded his group to a restaurant across the street from the historic depot.

The cafe was small, but tables had also been set up on the covered patio and it was here that Peter, Gina and the youngsters were seated after the obligatory wait in line. It was warmer there than in the air-conditioned dining room but climbing vines over latticework walls and strategically placed green plants provided a garden setting that kept it from being uncomfortable. Sonja and Johnny wanted hamburgers again, but this time Peter insisted they eat clam chowder and a fruit salad and refused to order them dessert. Even so they barely had time to eat and get back to the depot before the train pulled out and headed west.

Peter turned his and Johnny's seat around so the four of them could face each other on the return trip. But this time the children were too tired to argue and when they again reached Northspur both were curled up on a seat sound asleep, Sonja with her head in Gina's lap, and Johnny with his head in Peter's. Gina was aware of Peter's gaze on her, but she steadfastly refused to meet it as she sat absently watching the lush green forest rush by her window and stroking the blonde curls of the little girl in her lap.

As they slowed for the approach into Fort Bragg Peter finally spoke. "If I were an artist I'd paint you as a madonna. There's a radiance about you when you hold a sleeping child. Do you want babies of your own?"

The hypnotizing sway of the train combined with the steady clack-clack of the wheels had lulled Gina into letting down her guard and she spoke without thinking, or remembering her broken engagement. "Oh yes, but Stewart has a grown daughter. I don't think he wants more children."

Her eyes widened as she realized what she had said, and she saw the pain that flashed across his face as he winced. Then he quickly brought it under control and his features were expressionless as he said, "When you have children, my bewitching wife, it's not going to be Stewart Tobias who fathers them, it's going to be me and don't you forget it!"

Chapter Seven

For days Gina tried to erase Peter Van Housen from her thoughts, but his words kept vibrating through her mind. *When you have children it's going to be me who fathers them!* They brought alternating chills and hot flashes, and she cursed the day her ex-husband re-entered her life.

But there was the problem. Peter wasn't her *ex*-husband, he was a very real and *present* husband who fully intended to claim all his marital rights, and what terrified her during sleepless nights and anxious days was the humiliating knowledge that she wanted him to. Even after he'd deserted her more or less at the altar following the ceremony, had reviled her and refused to believe her plausible explanation, thought she was a liar and a cheat, the idea of bearing his children could still make her burn with longing for him.

She felt cheap and ashamed. He neither loved nor respected her, but she aroused his male passion with an uncomfortable urgency and he wanted it appeased.

In return he was willing to lower his high standards and allow her to keep the exalted Van Housen name and act as his wife; it was easier than looking around for an appealing young virgin with an impeccable pedigree. Virgins were in short supply these days!

Early the next morning Gina received a transatlantic phone call from her parents in Germany. Since Peter's assertion that he had written to her after their breakup seven years ago, she had tried several times to get in touch with Joe and Esther, but they had been on an extended vacation touring the countries of Europe in their tiny Volkswagen and had been unavailable. Now they had returned from their tour of Europe and wanted to share their experiences with their only child.

Joe spoke in his usual slow concise style, but Esther bubbled with excitement. She had enthusiastically described the sights in France, Italy and Austria before Gina was able to get in a word. "Mama, slow down a minute, there's something I want to ask you."

"Sure, honey," Esther said, "what is it?"

"Did I ever receive a letter from Peter Van Housen at your address after I started at the University of Maryland?"

For a moment there was silence on the other end of the line halfway around the world from Gina's apartment in Mendocino, and she held her breath and told herself it really didn't matter one way or the other.

"Why on earth do you want to bring that old scandal up, Ginny Lea," Esther answered sharply. "Haven't you suffered enough over that—that rat!"

It wasn't like her mother to be evasive. Gina's hands began to tremble. "Mama, please, it's important. I've seen Peter again and he tells me he wrote to me twice after we left San Francisco and asked that the letters be forwarded. Did they come to the house?"

"Well what if they did?" Her mother sounded petulant, like a child caught in a minor transgression. "He'd hurt you enough and you never did have any common sense where that young man was concerned. Your daddy had gone to a lot of trouble to get transferred clear across the country so you'd be away from him. He had no right to send you letters."

Gina could feel the blood drain from her face and she gripped the telephone. "Wh—what did you do with them?" she demanded, a little breathless with shock.

"Well I—I" Esther stammered. "Ginny Lea, I'm your mother and it was up to me to protect you from your carnal desires. Peter Van Housen was no good!"

"Mama," Gina said through gritted teeth. "What did you do with those letters? Do you still have them?"

Just because Peter wrote to her didn't necessarily mean he'd said anything she'd want to hear. Maybe he'd only wanted to harangue her further. If only her mother still had the letters she'd know for sure what was in them.

Her momentary surge of hope was dashed as Esther answered defiantly. "I burned them, that's what I did with them. Oh, don't worry, I didn't open them, I just took them down to the basement and threw them in the furnace. It was all for the best, Ginny Lea, you know it was—"

Gina hung up the phone.

The streets were crowded with the usual influx of weekend tourists later that morning when Gina took a break and walked around the corner and up the hill to the pastry shop for a loaf of warm, freshly baked bread. As she pushed open the door her senses were enticed by the savory aroma of baking cinnamon rolls, apple strudel, and pumpkin spice cake, and the empty feeling in her stomach reminded her that she hadn't eaten breakfast. She'd been too upset after the conversation with her mother to think of food, and now, several hours later, she was ravenous.

If she needed an excuse to indulge herself with fresh pastry and a cup of coffee she found it in Twyla who was standing at the glass counter eyeing the goodies. Gina walked over to stand beside her and said, "I'll buy the jelly-filled doughnuts and coffee if you have time to sit and talk for a few minutes."

Twyla assumed a pained expression. "It's bribery, pure and simple. You want to pick my brilliant mind and bask in my sunny disposition but never let it be said that I turned down a jelly doughnut. You get them and I'll get the coffee."

They settled down at a small round table on the sunny redwood deck at the front of the shop. Gina kept her left hand in her lap as she sipped her coffee and said, "I talked to my parents this morning. Mama admitted that I had received two letters from Peter shortly after we moved from San Francisco and she burned them without saying anything to me."

Twyla muttered a curse. "Did she read them first? Do you know what he said?"

"No." Gina ran her fingers through her short black hair. "I never would have believed Mama would do such a thing!"

Twyla shrugged. "You were very young at the time and you had been badly hurt. She probably thought she was protecting you."

"That's no excuse," Gina argued.

"Of course not, but there's nothing you can do about it now except maybe believe Peter when he says he's sorry."

Gina choked. "Sorry! He hasn't said he's sorry, only that he's willing to overlook my 'sexual experience' and continue with a loveless marriage."

"What are you going to do?" Twyla asked quietly.

"I'm going to fight for a divorce. I want to be free to get on with my life."

"Then why aren't you wearing Stewart's ring?"

The question was so unexpected that Gina could only stare before she lifted her left hand from her lap and glanced at her naked finger. "You noticed," she said stupidly.

Twyla nodded. "I noticed as soon as I saw you. I'm an artist, I'm trained to observe details. Do you want to tell me about it?"

Gina felt tears pressing against her eyeballs again and blinked to keep them back. Stewart had told her not to cry for him and she would honor his request. Hesitantly she gave Twyla the highlights of her evening with Stewart, omitting the more intimate moments. She finished by saying, "He's a very special kind of man and he was understanding and forgiving."

"And hurt," Twyla murmured.

Gina bowed her head. "Yes. I hate myself for what I've done to him." She took another sip of her coffee but left the doughnut untouched. "Twyla?" she hesitated then continued, "Will you go to Stewart? Sort of be a friend to him? He's going to need someone . . ."

"You have no right to ask that of me, Gina!" The anger in Twyla's tone was unmistakable. "I'm not in the market for your cast-off men!"

Gina was stunned that her friend would put that interpretation on her request and she gasped as she met Twyla's icy glare. "I didn't mean—" she began.

Twyla combed her long slender fingers through her loosely bound auburn hair. "I know," she said gruffly. "I overreacted, I'm sorry."

Gina looked at her friend thoughtfully. Twyla had never snapped at her like that before, and she certainly never lacked for male admirers. She turned down more dates than she accepted, so why was she so sensitive about offering Stewart a little moral support when he needed it? After all Twyla and Stewart had been friends before Gina ever arrived on the scene. In fact it was Twyla who introduced Stewart to Gina.

Gina frowned. Was she missing something here? Had Twyla and Stewart been more than just friends before Gina arrived?

No, she decided, there had never been any indication of a deeper, more intimate relationship between them. Twyla had been delighted when Stewart began seeing a lot of Gina, and later she had urged Gina to accept Stewart's proposal of marriage.

Twyla rummaged through her purse and lifted out a crumpled pack of cigarettes and her gold lighter, a sure sign she was troubled. Twyla seldom smoked unless she was upset, but then she lit one cigarette after another. Gina valued the older woman's friendship too highly to let it be strained by pride or lack of communication.

She took a deep breath and said, "Twyla, am I being dense? Did you and Stewart have something going between you before I—"

Twyla inhaled deeply and blew smoke into the clean fresh air before she answered. "Not really. Stewart and I started going together shortly after I came out here. It lasted for several months, but the wounds from his divorce were still raw, and I was determined not to get seriously involved again with any man. We drifted apart by mutual consent and I told myself I was being smart, independent, the liberated woman."

She took another puff of her cigarette. "I'm still telling myself that so let's change the subject."

"You're in love with him, aren't you?" Gina blurted.

"Gina . . ." Twyla snapped as she ground her cigarette out in the ashtray. "Yes, I suppose I am," she admitted, "but what I decide to do about it is strictly my own business. I don't need your advice or your interference."

Twyla rose and walked rapidly down the redwood steps and across the street.

Gina sat rooted to the chair, frozen with shock. Twyla was in love with Stewart! How could she, Gina, possibly not have known? She and Twyla were so close. Twyla, her art teacher, had been the rock that anchored her during those first grim months at the University of Maryland. Twyla, with her salty banter and warm strength, had provided the tormented teenager with a renewed assurance of her worth as a person and her talent as an artist. And how had Gina repaid her?

Gina shuddered and leaned back wearily. Why hadn't Twyla mentioned her brief affair with Stewart before? She'd simply introduced him as her friend and they'd never shown any romantic interest in each other. At least not in the three years Gina had been in Mendocino.

Stewart's legal residence was San Francisco. He owned a lovely home on a hill overlooking the city and until a year ago had only used the mountain home as a summer vacation cabin. It wasn't until he started courting Gina in earnest that he began spending both summer and winter there. Twyla had seemed genuinely pleased when they'd announced their engagement. Either she was an excellent actress or Gina had been blind and unfeeling.

She stood and gathered up her purse and the sack containing the still warm bread. No, she thought, it wasn't lack of perception on her part. Even with Gina, Twyla would reveal only the feelings she wanted revealed.

Gina spent the weekend trying to get in touch with Twyla, but she had apparently left town. Her house was locked, her telephone rang unanswered and at Gallery By The Sea her employees would only say that she had told them she wouldn't be in till Monday.

Gina alternately condemned and defended herself. Couldn't she ever do anything right? She'd only wanted to love Peter and he'd wound up hating her. She'd tried to spare Stewart and instead she'd hurt him dreadfully. She'd been insensitive to Twyla's feelings and had managed to alienate her closest friend.

Why was she making such a mess of everything? She'd made it plain to all concerned that she wanted to divorce Peter and marry Stewart. It's true she should have married him months ago, but the only reason she hadn't was because she'd been afraid to make herself that vulnerable to a man again. As for Peter, she'd left no doubt in his mind that she wanted to be free of him.

But if that was true why did she come running every time he beckoned, and why did she melt when he kissed her?

Her thoughts twisted and turned and spun in circles, leaving her with a pounding head, a queasy stomach and an overpowering desire to sleep and forget everything.

That was the reason she turned off her alarm on Sunday night and didn't waken until the doorbell chime lulled her to consciousness at ten o'clock on Monday morning. She jumped out of bed and felt dizzy, disoriented by the depth of her slumber. Who could that be? It was later than she usually slept but since it was her day off it wasn't likely to be anyone from the gallery.

She quickly pulled her blue- and white-checked cotton short robe over her matching nightie and glanced at herself in the mirror. Her eyes were heavy with sleep, her hair was disheveled and her lips looked full, as though they'd been thoroughly kissed. The doorbell chimed again and she walked through the apartment barefoot as she snapped shut the large ornamental snaps down the front of her robe.

The bell chimed a third time and she called, "I'm coming, I'm coming," as she swung the door open. "For heaven's sake must you make so much . . ."

The rest of the sentence died on her lips as her sleep-filled eyes finally focused on Peter Van Housen looking like one of those liquor ads picturing the handsome young executive at play, only he wasn't holding a drink in one hand.

He grinned. "Are you always so grumpy in the mornings?"

"Only when I'm wakened out of a sound sleep," she snapped. "What do you want?" She wished he wouldn't stand there looking so darn sexy in charcoal slacks and a blue pullover sweater that matched his eyes.

"For starters I'd like to come in . . ." he began, then his eyes narrowed and his expression hardened. "Or aren't you alone?"

"Of course I'm alone," she yawned. "I told you, I've been sleeping—"

The full meaning of his question finally hit her and she gasped. "My bed partners or lack of them are none of your business but yes, this morning I did happen to be sleeping alone. Now if you'll excuse me—"

She started to slam the door shut but he put his hand out and held it open as he walked into the narrow entryway and closed it behind him.

Gina turned to walk away but he caught her by the arms and held her while his gaze roamed over her face. "Your bed partners most definitely are my business, but my remark was uncalled for and I apologize. You aren't awake enough yet to fake this kind of innocent indignation."

He pulled her closer and the look on his face softened as he whispered, "Do I get a good morning kiss?"

The question was irrelevant because he didn't wait for an answer but covered her slightly parted lips with his own. Gina closed her eyes and swayed toward him as the impact of his nearness, his touch, swamped her. He smelled fresh, like the sea breeze, and although his lips were warm his face was cool and clean-shaven.

He turned his head slightly and murmured against the side of her mouth. "If I kiss you the way I want to I won't be able to stop. Will you let me share your bed this morning, Gina?"

She wanted to say yes, to press her body against his and feel the excitement of his hard maleness against her, to let him know by her rhythmic movements of her desire for him. Why not? Why shouldn't she let him make love to her when they both wanted it so much?

Because, you little idiot, a cold voice within her warned, *it wouldn't be making love, it would be having sex. Do you want that?*

Her body cried, *yes, anything,* but for once her mind won out. She pulled away from him and leaned against the wall, her hands clasped in front of her to still their trembling. She wasn't as successful with her voice and it quivered as she said, "I invited you to share my bed once and you told me I wasn't good enough to be your lover. Well now I don't want you, Peter, so keep your hands off me."

He watched her through half-closed eyes as he said, "You're lying to yourself, sweetheart, but I'll give you time to face the truth. Just don't make me wait too long, I don't think I can stand the frustration."

Since it was obvious that Peter had no intention of leaving just yet Gina asked him to make the coffee while she went back into the bedroom and dressed. It was a cool cloudy morning that smelled of rain and she pulled on a pair of purple corduroy slacks and a long-sleeved lilac blouse that did interesting things to her eyes. She looked a little more wide-awake after she bathed her face in cold water and she decided not to bother with make-up except for lip gloss in a shade called plum pink.

Peter had the coffee ready when she returned to the kitchen. She asked if he wanted breakfast and he explained that he'd had his some time ago, but if she could wait an hour or so longer to eat he'd take her out to lunch.

They took their coffee to the living room and sat

together on the sofa that faced the picture window with a full view of the bay. Gina's left hand lay in her lap as she held her mug in the other one. Peter took a swallow of his coffee then glanced over at her and stiffened. His fingers clamped around her wrist and he raised her hand as he said, "You're still not wearing your ring. Surely it doesn't take this long to tighten the stone."

Gina was so startled by his abrupt movement that she almost spilled her coffee, and she balanced her mug on the wide flat arm of the sofa before she spoke. "I—I gave it back to Stewart."

He also set his mug down and moved his hand so he could twine his fingers with hers. "Does this mean you're going to withdraw your petition for dissolution and come home with me where you belong?" His voice was tight, almost harsh.

Gina pulled her hand away from him. "No, it most certainly does not. It just means that I'm too fond of Stewart to keep him waiting months, or even years, while you play games with the law."

"*Fond* of him?" Peter sneered. "You were planning to marry him just because you were fond of him?"

Gina flared at Peter. "No way," she said heatedly. "I love Stewart. Oh, not with the wildness that I once loved you, but my feelings for Stewart are a lot deeper and more permanent and that's why I couldn't keep him in that purgatory you arranged for us."

Peter was watching her closely. "And was Stewart pleased? Did he thank you for releasing him from the engagement?"

She lowered her eyes. "No," she murmured as the memory of the scene two nights before brought back the pain. "No," she repeated, more to herself than to

Peter, "he didn't thank me. I hurt him badly, but do you know what he did? *He* comforted *me*. That's the kind of man Stewart is."

Peter rubbed the nape of his neck in a gesture of agitation. "Why did you need comforting, Gina?"

The tears she'd been so determined not to shed fell softly down her pale cheeks. "B-because I couldn't bear knowing what I was doing to him. I c-cried and he held me and told me to save my tears for myself because I'd need them if I got mixed up with you again."

She put her face in her hands and sobbed, and then she was in Peter's arms, crying into his shoulder. He held her gently, as though afraid of frightening her away, and murmured, "Why does it upset you so when you hurt Stewart? It doesn't bother you at all when you torment me."

Gina raised her head and looked at him, wide-eyed with amazement. "Torment you? I couldn't possibly torment you. You have to care about someone in order to be hurt by them and you never cared about me."

He closed his eyes and a spasm of emotion momentarily twisted his features as he pulled her roughly against him and buried his face in her dark hair. "You're a self-deceiving little fool if you believe that," he muttered thickly. "I nearly went out of my mind after Mel Calicutt identified that picture. For months I went around in a haze of agony. I don't even remember what I did during that time, only the pain."

His arms tightened around her and his voice took on a savage tone. "I'll never let you or any other woman do that to me again, Gina, so don't taunt me about not caring. You're right, I don't. I don't care about anything but protecting myself from your brand of loving."

Gina put her arms around Peter's neck and held him as she continued to sob. But her tears were no longer for Stewart; they were for the Ginny Lea and Peter of seven years ago who had been too young and immature to survive the holocaust that tore away their innocence and left them irreparably scarred.

Chapter Eight

For a long time they sat clasped in each other's arms, drawing comfort from their intimate but passionless contact. The only sound in the room was an occasional sob as Gina let her tears flow freely.

Finally the sobs stilled and the tears ceased. Peter reached in his pocket for a handkerchief and dabbed at her brimming violet eyes. "We're not going to cry anymore over the past, Gina," he said softly. "From now on we'll direct all our energy toward making a bright and happy future."

The corners of her mouth twitched in the beginnings of a smile and he bent his head and kissed her gently. Her hands stroked the back of his neck and he shivered and deepened the kiss, parting her lips and caressing them with his tongue. All of Gina's resistance had dissolved with her tears and she savored the taste and the feel and the scent of him.

He licked the moisture from her cheeks and brushed her closed eyelids with his lips as his hand cupped her breast through the silky material of her blouse. He tipped his head back and smiled at her. "You never used to wear a bra."

She smiled back. "I filled out as I got older."

"I'd noticed," he murmured as he stroked the taut fullness he cradled. "At eighteen you were a tantalizing adolescent with the promise of great beauty. You've fulfilled that promise, you're exquisite, but you've also matured into a woman of charm and passion. A woman I want for my own."

Like a valuable art object that you can brag about and show off to your friends, she thought bitterly as she undraped her arms from around his neck and placed her hands, palm up, against his chest to hold him away. "I don't want to be your woman, Peter," she said, and almost added, *I want to be your love,* but bit the words off in time.

He kissed the tip of her nose. "We'll see," he promised and released her. "Now go wash your face and put on a little make-up so people won't think I've been beating you and we'll go to lunch. I have something I want to show you."

They drove up Main Street and headed south on the coast highway. As they passed the small communities of Little River and Albion, Gina began to wonder where they were going since from there on the tiny towns were few and far between. She was just about to ask Peter when they came to the bottom of a gradual dip in the highway and he turned off onto a narrow road that led through the grove of pines and eucalyptus trees to a white sandy beach. Just before they drove out of the trees and onto the beach he turned again, this time into a long driveway that led to a rambling two story redwood home.

Peter stopped the car in front of the house and Gina turned to look at him. "Where are we? This is a private home, surely we're not having lunch here."

"Oh but we are," he said as he opened the door and got out.

He came around and took her hand as she stepped out of the car. The house was even larger than she'd first thought, and the forest setting with its smell of pine and cedar, its ground cover of low-growing fern and vines, and its towering trees was peaceful in its natural beauty.

Peter continued to hold her hand as they walked up the path strewn with pine needles and wood chips to the five wooden steps that led up to the covered porch which stretched halfway across the front of the building. Gina stood by speechless as he selected a key from his key ring and inserted it in the lock on the heavy oak door. It swung open without protest to reveal a brown-, tan- and gold- tiled entry hall.

She finally found her voice. "Peter, what are you doing?" she cried. "Whose house is this? You mustn't just walk in."

He grinned and once more took her by the hand and pulled her inside. "Not to worry, love. Hasn't it occurred to you that since I have a key I must also have a right to entry?"

She was too busy gaping to answer. To her right was a library with floor-to-ceiling books lining its walls, to her left was a spacious kitchen with sparkling maple cabinets and sunny yellow appliances. Both rooms opened wide onto the entryway but could be closed off with hidden sliding doors. Straight ahead of her was a green-carpeted living room with a wall of glass that looked out over the blue ocean with its foaming whitecaps that washed up on the vast expanse of silvery beach.

Gina walked over to the wall and gasped. Directly outside was a redwood deck that was accessible through a sliding glass door. There were deeply padded lounges, a large round umbrella table with four white wrought-iron chairs, and an electric barbecue grill built into a brick fireplace. There was plenty of room for more furniture should the need arise.

Peter came up behind her and put his arms around her waist. "Do you like it?" There was a note of urgency in his voice, as if her answer was most important.

"Oh, I love it!" she exclaimed. "That panoramic view of the ocean and the beach is magnificent! Who is the lucky person who has the incredible good fortune to own this place?"

He pulled her back against him and rubbed his cheek in her hair. "We do," he said simply.

Gina felt as though an electric current had run through her and she stiffened. "I beg your pardon?" she choked out.

"We own it, Gina, you and I together."

She pulled out of his embrace and walked a few steps away before turning to face him. "That's not possible," she muttered. "There's no way I could ever buy half interest in this property."

He gestured impatiently. "Don't be dense, I bought it and had it put in both our names. It's our home, yours and mine, and I want you to live here with me."

"Aren't you assuming a great deal?" she said angrily. "You had no right—"

"I'm not assuming anything and I have every right," he interrupted. "Are you forgetting that we're married? According to California's community property laws the house would be half yours whether I registered it that way or not. So is everything else I've bought in the past seven years."

"But we've never—" Gina began.

"I'm uncomfortably aware of what we've never done," Peter snapped, "and I intend to remedy that little oversight just as soon as I can persuade you to cooperate, but meanwhile our lack of cohabitation doesn't affect your rights as my wife."

He sighed and ran his hand through his thick blond hair. "Let's not quarrel, honey," he said softly. "I don't expect you to move in immediately. I'll give you time to consider it, and there's something else you should know. If our marriage is ever dissolved the house will be all yours, no strings attached."

Gina opened her mouth to protest, but he held up a silencing hand. "It's all arranged, I couldn't change it if I wanted to so don't argue."

Gina was stunned. Why was Peter doing this? He'd been so sure that she'd only married him for his money, now he was forcing this valuable property on her. It must be worth hundreds of thousands of dollars, possibly even more on today's market. He was making her financially independent even if she divorced him without ever having lived with him.

She cleared her throat but even so her voice sounded raspy. "I don't want expensive gifts from you."

"Then we'll call it a settlement. You've been my wife for a long time now and never once have you asked me for money, so let's say I owe it to you." He made a tentative effort to smile. "Now, do you want to see the rest of your house or shall I have Mrs. Webster serve lunch first?"

Gina was surprised. "You mean you have a house-keeper out here?"

Peter's smile was brighter this time. "Sure, and a caretaker too. Margaret and Bud Webster. They live in an apartment on the other side of the kitchen. Look, why don't you make yourself comfortable and I'll go tell her we're ready to eat. We can tour the house afterwards."

Gina nodded and walked toward a cream-colored velvet sofa. "Do you have a bar?" she asked. "I think I need a drink."

"You can have anything you want, sweetheart," Peter answered. "All you have to do is ask. I'll get it for you as soon as I talk to Mrs. Webster."

Gina settled herself on the long comfortable sofa and looked around her. The room was an enormous rectangle with a natural stone fireplace at one end. The other end was furnished as a dining room with a solid oak table, chairs and china cabinet while in between were two separate furniture groupings of sofas, upholstered chairs, coffee tables, lamps, etc. The walls were paneled with exposed beam ceilings. She was awed by the size and the opulence.

Peter was back almost immediately. "Mrs. Webster says lunch will be served in a few minutes. She has everything ready, it only needs warming," he said as he walked toward her.

He stopped in front of her and reached out for her hand. "Come, I'll show you where the bar is."

They walked hand in hand into a hall and entered another wide, open doorway to the left into another sitting room, this one smaller and more intimate. It shared the rustic stone fireplace with the living room, but on this side it was smaller, cozier. A large picture window overlooked the ocean and the furniture was less formal, more inviting. Gina loved it on sight and Peter told her it was called the family room.

He walked to the bar and poured them each a Scotch and soda. She accepted her drink and sat down on the burgundy velour sofa facing the unlit fireplace. He followed and sat down beside her as she turned to him and asked, "Peter, how did you find this house? Surely you didn't have it built?"

He took a swallow of his whiskey before he answered. "No, I didn't build it, but it's only a couple of years old. The man who built it was an actor who had the lead in a brand new television series. Unfortunately it was cancelled after the first year and he hasn't worked steady since. He couldn't meet the mortgage payments so he put it on the market. I was looking for a place to buy up here so—"

"Why?" asked Gina.

Peter quirked one dark brown eyebrow. "Why? You know why. Because I knew I'd never entice you into leaving that gallery of yours and moving back to San Francisco. This way you're only a fifteen-minute drive from Mendocino and I can move my base of operations up here. I'll have to spend some time in San Francisco but—"

"Peter, stop that! I told you—"

He leaned over and kissed her full on the mouth, effectively cutting off her indignant tirade.

Margaret Webster was a middle-aged woman with bright hazel eyes and a warm smile. She was medium height with a matronly figure and long brown hair streaked with gray which she wore braided and wrapped around her head. Peter introduced Gina as his wife and if Mrs. Webster was surprised she didn't show it.

Lunch was served on the deck overlooking the beach and the ocean. The sun had come out and since they were situated in a hollow the breeze went right over them and it was warm and pleasant in the fresh sea air. They ate chunky homemade vegetable soup, shrimp salad and hot yeast rolls to the accompaniment of the swishing sound of waves rolling gently onto the sand.

Gina pushed her empty salad plate away and sighed with contentment. "Margaret Webster is a jewel of a cook," she told Peter. "Don't ever let her get away from you."

Peter leaned back in his chair and grinned lazily. "No chance of that. The pay and working conditions are too good."

He frowned as she stood and started stacking the dirty dishes. "There's no need for you to do that," he insisted. "Mrs. Webster's working conditions are good but not that good. She *is* expected to clear off the table after meals."

Gina laughed as she picked up a tray from the serving counter and began putting the dishes on it. "You may be used to being waited on, but I'm not. There's no reason for her to come out here to get these when I can just as well take them in."

She picked up the tray and walked inside with it, leaving Peter sputtering behind her.

Mrs. Webster was as indignant as Peter at the idea of Gina bringing the dirty dishes into the kitchen. "It's my job, ma'am, there's no need for you to trouble yourself," she scolded gently.

Gina thanked her for the delicious meal and asked

directions to the bathroom where she combed her hair and repaired her lipstick before rejoining Peter on the deck.

He had moved from his seat at the table and was sprawled out on one of the wide redwood loungers that was padded with thick foam rubber covered in heavy apple green toweling.

He watched her as she walked across the living room and out the sliding glass door, closing it behind her. He looked relaxed and content, and she almost expected to hear him purr. Instead he held out his hand to her. "Come here," he invited.

She eyed him warily. "What do you want?"

He patted the space beside him. "I want you to sit with me."

She stood where she was. "There isn't room."

"Of course there is," he said. "Come on, I'm not going to bite you, tempting though the thought is."

He looked so appealing, almost boyish, pleading with those incredibly blue eyes. Why didn't she have the good sense to stay away from him? she wondered as she moved slowly in the direction of the lounger. There were plenty of chairs; the smart thing to do would be to change direction and sit in one out of touching distance from him, but she didn't. She continued in a straight course until she was standing beside him.

Again he patted the narrow space next to him and reluctantly she sat down as he reclined beside her. He picked up her hand and brought it to his lips, then turned it over and licked the palm, sending shivers through her in all directions. She tried to pull away, but he moved it to his smooth cheek and rubbed the back of it gently against him in a caressing movement.

He was behaving like a child starved for affection

and without being conscious of willing it her hand began to move on its own. She stroked upward to his brow and smoothed back an errant lock of golden hair. It was springy, alive under her fingertips, and she threaded her fingers through it, carefully massaging his head as she explored the back and sides of it.

She wasn't aware of his arms around her until she felt herself being guided downward and she twisted around so that she could stretch out beside him. He held her securely but without pressure against the length of him and she had no wish to resist, instead she relaxed with her head on his shoulder.

They lay quietly for a while and listened to the whisper of the breeze in the trees and the lapping of the surf on the shore. Finally Gina broke the silence. "This is the most incredible place. You enter the house from the forest and exit onto the beach."

"Do you like it?" Peter asked lazily.

"It's straight out of a dream," she answered. "The type of home women long for but never expect to have."

"Will you live here with me?"

She found that it took all of her resolve to answer that question with a whispered, "no," instead of the insistent *yes* that hovered on her tongue.

He sighed and lowered his head to kiss the top of hers. "If I agree to live with you as brother and sister, to give you your own room with a key to lock it against me, will you stay?"

Gina tilted her head back and looked up at him in amazement. "That's ridiculous!" she yipped. "We'd be in bed together before the first night was over and you know it."

He chuckled. "I'm afraid you're right, but my intentions were honest."

She settled her head back on his shoulder and put her arms around his waist. He cradled her lovingly but made no attempt to kindle the desire that burst into flame so easily between them. She was surprised by his restraint, but she realized that it was probably a self-protective measure. He was very male and programmed to be easily and urgently aroused. It must have been even more agonizing for him to be stopped abruptly at the last moment than it was for her.

That thought took her back to his offer to live with her without sex. Why did he propose that? She knew it wasn't done capriciously or to tease. He'd been serious, but why? He wanted her, that much was obvious. He'd always wanted her, even enough to marry her against all the opposition, the difference in their backgrounds, and his own good sense. Now after a separation of seven years he still wanted her, but this time he'd made no pretense of being in love with her. He didn't care about her, he'd told her that only a few hours ago, and still he offered to leave her untouched if that's what it took to get her to live with him.

It didn't make sense. Nothing made sense anymore. Here she was curled up in an intimate embrace with a man she was supposed to hate and her only regret was that she couldn't lie like this with him forever.

His hold on her had relaxed slightly and his heart beat in a strong steady rhythm beneath her ear. He was asleep. She turned her head carefully and kissed the hollow at the base of his throat then wiggled into a more comfortable position against him. He grunted contentedly and she closed her eyes and let the lullaby of the ocean rock her to sleep.

* * *

At first she was only aware of the tingle that caused the muscles in the pit of her stomach to tighten, but as she struggled upward through the warm drowsiness she felt the hand stroking her bare breast and the lips that were nuzzling the sensitive side of her neck. Her own hand moved against a rough material that felt like fine spun wool which encased a solid substance that twitched under her touch.

Gina opened her eyes and gazed into Peter's deep blue ones, smoky now with passion. She blinked and looked down at where her hand rested just below his hip on the outside of his thigh. The material she felt was his gray slacks, and under them the muscles of his thigh were definitely twitching.

She removed her hand, confused and embarrassed, but he left off fondling her breast to put her hand back to its original position. "Leave it there," he said. "I like it."

She liked it too, and she liked it even more when he returned his attention to the rapidly hardening nipple on the firm white mound he'd been caressing. She realized that he'd unbuttoned her blouse and unfastened the front clasp on her mauve satin bra. For a moment she was sorry. It meant that they could no longer lie quietly in each other's arms. That soon, very soon, she'd have to stop him and experience the pain of unfulfillment all over again.

He dipped his head and taunted her breast with his lips before taking the dark, throbbing tip in his mouth. The tingle in her stomach had spread down her legs and unconsciously her fingers began to knead his thigh. He moaned with pleasure and moved his leg over both of hers as he pushed on her hips bringing her against him in such a way that she was shatteringly aware of his urgent need for her.

"Gina. Oh Gina," he murmured huskily. "I want you so badly." His hand went to the zipper on her purple corduroys. "I didn't mean for this to happen, but I made the mistake of going to sleep, letting down my defenses. When I woke up and found you in my arms I—I couldn't help it."

He unzipped her zipper and slipped his hand under her slacks to rest on her quivering stomach. His breathing was ragged as he sought and found her eagerly parted lips. She put her arms around his neck and pulled him even closer as her tongue met his. Her trembling body was on fire and she had no thought of stopping him. She couldn't if she wanted to and she didn't want to.

He rolled over until his body nearly covered hers and she welcomed him with her mouth, and her hands and her whispered words of wanting. They were both so overpowered by the sensations that flowed between them that they were aware of nothing but the throbbing urgency of their terrible need to be one in body as well as soul.

It wasn't surprising that they didn't hear the commotion inside the house or the heavy glass door being slid open. It wasn't until two childish voices yelling "Uncle Peter, Uncle Peter, surprise!" burst through the haze of passion that they came to the appalling realization that they were no longer alone.

Gina and Peter tore themselves apart and Gina, who had her back to the house, looked over her shoulder to see Johnny and Sonja being held back by their mother, Peter's sister Lillian. Behind them were an older but still recognizable Hans and Bertha Van Housen: Peter's parents, who stood rigid, their faces a study of shock and embarrassment.

Chapter Nine

Gina's entire body burned with guilt and humiliation and she instinctively turned again toward Peter and buried her face in his sweater-clad chest as she held her gaping blouse together with shaking hands. Oh dear Lord, how could she have been so wanton as to let Peter practically undress her right here in the open in broad daylight? And the position they'd been in! It must have looked obscene, and to think that the children . . .

Peter swore and held her close, stroking his fingers through her hair in a comforting gesture as he barked grimly, "What are you doing here?"

Gina recognized Lilly's voice although it had lost its usual confident timbre. "Pete, I'm sorry. Mom and Dad wanted to see the house. We had no idea—look, we'll wait for you in the library."

Gina heard the children protest as Lilly ordered them into the house *immediately,* along with the sound of scuffling feet before the glass door slid closed. She was shivering uncontrollably, not from cold but from shattered nerves. Peter's arms tightened about her and he spoke forcefully. "Gina, it's all right. We've done nothing wrong. We're married and we're in our own home. We have a perfect right to make love anywhere we want to on our own property."

"I want to die!" Her voice was jerky and somewhat muffled in his chest.

He nuzzled her temple. "Don't talk like that," he said harshly. "They had no right to come bursting in that way. I didn't invite them here. Come now, pull yourself together and we'll go in and see what they want."

"No!" It was more a scream than a statement. "I couldn't face them! I don't ever want to see them again. Take me home, Peter. Oh please, take me home."

He gripped her by the shoulders and shook her gently. "Stop that, sweetheart, I'm not going to take you anywhere. You are home, and as soon as we get you all buttoned and snapped back up we're going to go in there and establish that fact once and for all."

He pulled the front ends of her bra together and fastened them, then started buttoning her blouse. She made no move to help but sat shaking her head from side to side. "No, Peter, there's no reason for me to face your family. They never did like me, and now they have even more reason not to. They must think I'm no better than a streetwalker!"

He clapped his hand across her mouth and now he was really angry. "That's enough! I'll not tolerate that kind of talk."

He removed his hand and started tucking her blouse under her opened slacks. "If you don't like the way my parents treat you then do something about it," he advised her. "Tell them to either shape up or get out."

Gina stared at him uncomprehendingly. "But—but they're your family."

He shook his head. *You're* my family, and this is your house. You don't have to put up with anything in it that you don't want to." He grinned teasingly. "Except from me, of course."

The teasing smile disappeared as quickly as it had come. "I'm serious, Gina," he said. "Seven years ago you were too young and immature to stand up to Dad and Mother and I tried to protect you, but now you're a full-grown woman, and a feisty one. You can and do fight your own battles. I should know, I've got the scars to prove it. Now, we're going in there and confront them and if they give you any trouble light in to them the way you do to me. I guarantee they'll back down."

She brushed his hands away from their fumbling attempts to close the zipper on her slacks and fastened it herself. "Why should they do that? You never do," she questioned.

He kissed her on the tip of her nose. "Oh, but I do, love. You slash me to ribbons every time we get together, but I keep coming back for more." He frowned, "I can't think what's wrong with me. No one has ever treated me the way you do and been given a second chance."

Gina was still cradled full length against Peter in a protective embrace, but she was calmer now. Her hands trembled but she wasn't shaking as violently as she had been. For a moment she was tempted to do as Peter asked, march in the house and tell his parents and sister that they could either accept her on her own terms or leave. It was a huge temptation. Hans and

Bertha Van Housen had considered her so totally unacceptable for their youngest son that they hadn't even taken her seriously until Peter announced that he was going to marry her. After that they'd tried every way they could to break it up, and she knew they'd been delighted when their appraisal of her was apparently vindicated and Peter left her without even consummating the marriage.

Oh yes, it was tempting to throw a few of their own rocks back at them, but it was too late now. There would just be a painful scene and they would still win. She had no intentions of living here with Peter as his wife, so it would be childish to stir up trouble in the Van Housen household.

She rolled away from him and stood on her still rubbery legs. She straightened her rumpled clothes and said, "I don't want to confront your family, Peter, there's nothing to be gained. I'll never live here with you. You can delay my petition for dissolution from being heard for a while but when we finally go to court I'll win and you know it. Now I'm going home. If you won't take me I'll walk into Albion and hire someone to drive me to Mendocino."

She turned and started to walk toward the redwood steps that led to the beach but Peter quickly stepped in front of her and held her by both arms. "Oh no, Gina, you're not going to run away again!"

"Again!" she raged. "It wasn't me who ran away after we were married! You walked out and left me to face my family and friends, not to mention the newspaper reporters and curious bystanders. I didn't run away, I was forced to move out of San Francisco in order to preserve my sanity. Now step aside and let me go."

His fingers tightened painfully on her upper arms

and for a few seconds he glared at her with a rage almost equal to her own. Then, unexpectedly, his grim features softened and he dropped his hands from her arms and nodded with a weary resignation. "All right, I'll take you home," he said quietly and led her down the steps onto the beach and around the side of the house to his ebony Jaguar.

He helped her into the passenger seat, then went around the car and slid under the steering wheel. "Hadn't you better tell your parents where you're going?" she asked.

He inserted the key and turned it and the powerful engine roared to life. "I didn't invite them here and they didn't tell me they were coming. I don't owe them any explanations," he answered and threw the gear shift into reverse.

They drove the fifteen scenic miles in silence and when they stopped in front of her building he didn't get out of the car but reached across her and opened her door. As she turned to step out she said, "Goodbye, Peter" and as she shut the door he murmured, "Good-bye," and then he was gone.

Sleepless nights were getting to be a habit with Gina. She'd had a lot of them since Peter came back into her life and this one was no exception. The events of the day kept filtering through her mind over and over, giving her no peace.

Why was he so intent on holding her to wedding vows that had no meaning? Why would he spend a fortune on a house in the hope of enticing her to live there with him? He wanted a wife, but he could have his pick of any number of women in his own social and financial set, women who met all the strict qualifications for being a Van Housen bride. He said he saw no reason to look for another wife when he already had one, but he also said he would never love her.

No matter how many times she went over it it always came back to just one thing. Physical attraction. He wanted her, needed her, as much as she wanted and needed him, but that wasn't enough for her. She knew now that she loved him, it would be silly of her to deny it, and that love made her frighteningly vulnerable. If she gave in and went to live with him as his wife he would eventually break her heart. He'd done that to her once, she'd never survive a repeat performance.

She thrashed around on her disheveled bed trying to find a comfortable position. Even though she'd taken a warm soapy shower she still felt Peter's hands on her, his mouth nuzzling, nipping, caressing. She pounded her pillow with disgust.

Maybe she should go to bed with him! Get it over with. Appease the tormenting ache that caused them both so much anguish. Surely once they'd made love they would get it out of their systems. It was just the unknown, the mystery, the thrill of the chase that made it all so exciting. Once they'd ended the chase, solved the mystery, explored the unknown it would cease to beckon and lure.

Or would it? For him, maybe, but not for her. Gina knew herself and her obsession for Peter too well. Once he made her truly his she would be bonded to him for life. It wasn't fair, it wasn't even fashionable, but it was a flaw in her character. She was a one-man woman and that man was Peter Van Housen!

It was late the next morning when she looked up from the cash register where she was making change for a customer and saw Lillian Van Housen Wilcox, Peter's sister, standing in front of her.

Gina had only gotten an impression of Lilly yesterday when she'd glimpsed her in that hideously embarrassing moment. But now she was standing not three feet away and Gina could see that the past seven years had been kind. Lilly had changed little. Her blonde hair, only slightly darker than Peter's, was worn short in tight little curls close to her head instead of shoulder-length as it used to be. Her slender figure was still girlish and her clear pale complexion unlined. She wore a leaf green slack suit that accentuated the green flecks in her blue Van Housen eyes. At age thirty-seven she looked ten years younger.

Gina's eyes widened with surprise and it was Lilly who spoke. "Hello, Ginny Lea."

The warm flush of embarrassment flooded through Gina as she remembered the intimate scene Lilly and her parents had witnessed the day before in Peter's home. She lowered her gaze and hoped her face wasn't too rosy as she said, "Hello, Lilly."

She couldn't think of anything else to say, and Lilly seemed to be having the same problem as they stood looking at each other across the counter.

Lilly was the first to rally. "It's important that I talk to you, Ginny Lea. It's nearly noon, will you be free for lunch soon?"

The last thing Gina wanted to do was talk to Peter's sister, or any other member of his family, but there didn't seem to be any way to avoid it and not be childish. She glanced at her watch and said, "My assistant will be along shortly. If you'll meet me here in half an hour we can have lunch upstairs in my apartment."

Lilly nodded. "Fine. I'll bring sandwiches from the local deli if you'd like to furnish the coffee."

Fortunately a group of tourists who were apparently traveling together wandered in a few minutes later and were still there asking questions and making small purchases when Lilly came back. Gina hadn't had time to worry about why her sister-in-law wanted to talk to her, but she made up for that oversight when Lilly reappeared. What kind of scene was she in for now?

They went upstairs to the apartment and Gina made coffee and arranged on a platter the ham and turkey sandwiches Lilly had provided. They made inconsequential small talk until they were ready to eat, then they took their food to the kitchen table and sat down. Lilly picked up her ham sandwich, looked at it and then laid it back on her plate as she said, "So you're the 'Aunt Gina' who made such an impression on my kids when Peter brought them up here for the Skunk Train ride."

Gina looked at her in amazement. "You mean you didn't know?"

Lilly shook her head. "I had no idea. I thought it was just some girl Peter had taken a fancy to. Remember, I knew you as Ginny Lea."

"But didn't he tell you that we ran into each other at Cynthia Tobias's wedding?"

Again Lilly picked up her sandwich. "He didn't tell me anything, but it's not altogether his fault. Dad and Mother have been on an Alaskan cruise and I don't see a lot of Pete. He didn't say a word about you when he made arrangements with Henry and me to take Johnny and Sonja to Fort Bragg. I thought it was a little odd that he'd want to take the kids on an outing for a couple of days, but he's always been good with them so I didn't question his motives."

She took a bite of the sandwich and then muttered around it. "Apparently I should have."

Gina ignored the somewhat bitter remark as she said, "Didn't your parents know about me either?"

"Nope, they've only just returned from their cruise."

Gina fingered her turkey sandwich. "Then it must have been a surprise as well as an embarrassment when you—uh—walked in on us yesterday."

"Wrong," Lilly said with a sigh. "You had your back to us and we were all too flustered to look closely anyway. None of us knew you had come back into Peter's life until he came home after bringing you back here and told us so."

She shuddered. "I've never seen my brother so mad! He was breathing enough fire and smoke to ignite the whole forest, and his language . . ." She rolled her eyes. "Mother nearly had an attack of the vapors and Dad looked positively apoplectic." She grinned. "Peter even used words I'd never heard before. Anyway, when he finally calmed down a little he told us the whole story."

"Did he tell you he's contesting my petition for dissolution and wants me to live with him?" Gina asked.

"Oh yes," Lilly answered. "When he dropped that little bombshell Mom went into a decline and Dad had to take her upstairs and put her to bed." She thought a moment then added, "She managed to recover just before dinner was served."

It sounded as though Lilly was making light of the situation, but Gina couldn't be sure. She didn't know Peter's sister that well. Seven years ago Lilly had kept her disapproving distance from Gina.

She frowned and asked, "Is your mother all right?"

Lilly chuckled. "Mom has the constitution of an ox, she'll outlive us all. Mainly because she keeps the rest of us in a constant state of anxiety with her fainting spells and temper tantrums. She knows exactly when to pout, sigh, cry, faint or yell in order to get her own way. It works with everyone in the family but Peter. He simply ignores her and does as he pleases, and I think she loves him most of all."

Gina had been munching on her sandwich but now she laid it back on her plate and faced Lilly squarely. "Okay, Lil," she said, "I know your parents neither like nor approve of me, but what about you. Are you my friend or my enemy?"

This time there was no levity in Lilly's tone. "That depends on you, Gina. You really did a job on Peter seven years ago. For a while I was afraid he was going to crack up. I can't forgive you for that, and now you're back and it's starting all over again."

She shifted in her chair and when she spoke again it was a challenge. "Just what do you want from my brother?"

Gina sipped her coffee and was careful not to let the cup shake in her hands. "The only thing I want from Peter is my freedom," she answered. "During all those years I thought the marriage had been annulled, I was even making plans to marry again. Now Peter's decided he wants me after all and is fighting my efforts to be free."

Lilly spread her hands in a vague gesture. "Did you ever love him, Gina?"

Gina's shoulders slumped. It would do no good to go over her side of the story again, the Van Housen clan believed exactly what they wanted to and refused to let facts confuse the issue.

She set down her coffee cup and said, "I've always loved Peter. It was his love for me that wasn't strong enough and now it's dead, buried, forgotten." She grimaced. "Tell your mother to stop wasting time on fainting spells and find a suitable replacement for me and he'll be happy to let me go. All he wants is a wife and he doesn't care who it is as long as she's willing to give him children and be presentable to his business associates."

Lilly brushed bread crumbs from her finger tips and looked at Gina with disgust. "Are you really as blind as you seem or is it all an act? Peter's hurting bad and not because he wants just any old wife. When he confronted us yesterday afternoon he looked the same way he did when he came back to San Francisco and found you gone. I worried about him then and I worry about him now. The first thing he did when he came into the house yesterday was pour himself a glass of whiskey and he's been drinking steadily ever since."

Gina blanched. "I find that hard to believe," she said. "Peter's never been a heavy drinker."

"Believe it," Lilly muttered. "He drank all through dinner and the evening last night, and when he got up this morning he was hung over so he started drinking again. That's why I'm here."

Gina looked up, startled, as Lilly continued. "If he wants to get smashed in his own home there's not much anyone can do about it, but he insists he's going to drive back to San Francisco this afternoon and that I can't allow. Someone has to stop him, and I'm afraid you're the only one who can do it."

A germ of fear planted itself in Gina's mind and crept stealthily along her nerves as she pictured the narrow two-lane coast highway twisting and turning high above the pounding waves of the ocean where they slammed against the rocky cliffs below. "Surely," she gasped, "he's not intending to drive Highway 1!"

"No," said Lilly quickly. "He'll go the inland route,

but don't forget he has to cross the mountain range to get to Highway 101."

The fear in Gina did not abate as her mind's eye reviewed the mountain road, broad at some stretches, but narrow and dangerous at others. The high drop-offs were picturesque but lethal to anyone in a car that went over the side.

She felt panicky as she stood up. "I can't believe that I'll have any influence with Peter," she said, "but if he insists on leaving I'll go with him and drive."

As they sped down the highway toward Peter's home Gina began having second thoughts about her impulsive actions. Lilly was driving Peter's Jaguar and when Gina questioned her she explained that her father had taken his grandchildren to a movie matinee in Fort Bragg so she'd borrowed the Jag from Peter on the excuse that she had to go to Mendocino for groceries. She knew that if she had his car he couldn't start out for San Francisco until she got back.

Gina was terrified at the thought of Peter driving the car, but how on earth could she stop him? He'd been furious with her yesterday and it wasn't likely he felt any more kindly toward her today. If she asked him not to leave he'd probably do it just to spite her, especially if he was drinking. She'd never seen Peter drunk except two days after the wedding when they'd found him passed out in a waterfront bar. Even so, he had been pretty well sobered up by the time she'd talked to him; her father had insisted on that.

Even more daunting than the thought of arguing with Peter again was the prospect of facing Hans and Bertha Van Housen. Peter's parents were forceful, intimidating personalities who would use any means to discredit her in the eyes of their youngest son. She shivered. She must be an idiot to deliberately subject herself to them!

Lilly brought the car to a stop in front of the house and turned off the motor. As she started to open the door she turned to Gina and, as though reading her mind, said, "If Dad and Mother give you a bad time just ignore them. I'll deflect them. You try to get Peter to stop drinking and forget about driving to San Francisco."

Mrs. Webster answered the door and smiled a welcome at Gina as the two women stepped into the entryway. Gina followed Lilly into the living room where Bertha was reclining on the cream-colored velvet sofa with one arm over her eyes.

Peter's mother removed the sweater-covered arm from her aging blue eyes and looked at her daughter. "Lilly," she scolded, "where have you been? Peter's been grumbling for the past hour because you were gone so long with the car."

She looked past Lilly and for the first time saw Gina standing there. Her jaw tightened and she sat up with surprising grace for one so heavy. Bertha Van Housen was of medium height but considerably overweight, although she was always carefully corseted and fashionably gowned. Today she wore a navy blue jersey dress with white polka dots and had added a navy blue hand-knit sweater to ward off the chill of the ocean breeze. Her hair, once blonde but now white, was worn in a short, lightly curled style that was becoming to her round face.

She glared at Gina and spoke in a glacial tone. "So you're back, Virginia Lea. We'd hoped you'd have the good grace to stay out of Peter's life, but apparently that was too much to expect."

Seven years ago Gina had longed for acceptance by the wealthy Van Housen family and would have been crushed by such a stinging rejection, but now all she felt was contempt and possibly a little pity for this arrogant, self-centered woman. She locked her gaze with Bertha's and said, "It is a little much to expect, I agree, since I happen to be Peter's wife and this is my home. Now, if you'll excuse me I must talk to my husband."

She walked off leaving mother and daughter staring after her in shocked silence.

Gina found Peter in the family room standing at the picture window looking out at the ocean. He had his back to her and mistook her for Lilly as he said, "It's about time you got back with my car. You knew I was anxious to get started for San Francisco."

He turned and saw her framed in the doorway. The ice in his highball glass tinkled, an indication that his hand was not altogether steady. For a moment he just looked at her, and when he spoke it was not a welcome. "Well, to what do I owe the honor of your presence?" he mocked. "I thought you couldn't wait to get rid of me."

He didn't invite her to come in and sit down but took a swallow of his drink without breaking eye contact with her.

Gina was looking into the light from the window and couldn't see Peter's face clearly, but his tone indicated his disgust. Perhaps she deserved it. Maybe she should have stayed and done battle with the senior Van Housens yesterday. All she'd gained by running was Peter's ire and a few hours postponement of the inevitable. Well, she'd overcome the first hurdle, Bertha, so she might as well tackle Peter too.

She walked across the heavily carpeted floor to

stand in front of him. He was wearing jeans and a white cotton T-shirt and beneath the day's growth of dark golden stubble his face was gray and drawn. He raised his glass and clanked the ice cubes together, deliberately this time, as he taunted, "You should have let me know you were coming, I'd have spiffed up for you. You can't really blame me for not expecting you—it's the first time *you've* ever come to *me.*"

He took another swallow of whiskey then looked at the meager contents left in the glass. "I'm going to have a refill," he said. "Can I fix you something?"

Without answering Gina reached out and took the glass from his hand. "Go sit down, I'll fix it for you," she said and headed toward the bar.

Peter didn't move but watched her as she found a bottle of club soda and poured it into the whiskey until the glass was again full. He made a face and muttered, "That wasn't exactly what I had in mind."

She smiled as she came toward him with the drink. "That's what you're going to get as long as I'm tending bar."

He took the glass from her and moved to the couch. "Remind me to have you replaced, *pronto,*" he grumbled as he sat down.

Peter leaned his head against the back of the velour sofa and closed his eyes, and for a few minutes neither of them spoke. It was impossible to tell how much he had been drinking by his actions or his speech, but he looked ill and Gina suspected he was the type who got sick instead of drunk.

Without moving or opening his eyes he said, "You might as well tell me what you want. I know you didn't come here just to sit beside me on the couch."

Actually, she'd been enjoying the quiet closeness and was fighting the urge to move closer and take his hand. He seemed to like to have her touch him, but that always started up another whole train of thought that was best left dormant.

Instead she answered factually. "Lilly brought me. She said you were drinking too much and talking about driving to San Francisco and she wanted me to stop you."

He muttered an oath. "I see my big sister is still meddling in my life. I wish she'd back off and leave me alone."

"It's only because she loves you that she worries."

He rubbed his forehead with the back of his hand. "I'm glad to hear somebody loves me."

He sounded so bleak, as though he really was lonely and unloved. Gina bit her lip but the words came anyway. "Do you want me to love you, Peter?"

He turned his head toward her then and opened his eyes. For a second she thought she saw a flicker of—yearning? but it was replaced by a veiled scrutiny before she could be sure. "You know what I want," he said impatiently, "I want *you.*"

Gina tried to ignore the hurt and told herself that she deserved it. She should have known better than to ask that question. He didn't want her love, only her body.

She shifted uncomfortably and changed the subject. "Have you had lunch?"

He took a drink of his whiskey-flavored soda. "No."

"Did you eat breakfast?"

"I didn't feel like eating," he said. "I had a drink instead."

She frowned. "How about dinner last night?"

"No Mama," he mimicked, "I didn't have my

spinach last night either. What difference does it make? Who appointed you my keeper?"

"Lilly did," she snapped, "and it will make a big difference if you don't want to be violently ill very shortly."

He groaned. "I suspect that I will be anyway so why bother to eat? It'll just make it that much worse when it happens."

She felt a wave of sympathy tinged with annoyance as she got up and walked over to stand in front of him. "Come to the kitchen with me and I'll fix you a sandwich."

She put out her hand to help him up, but when he took it he gave a tug and she landed in his lap instead. He gripped her tightly so she couldn't slip away from him as he said, "Why should you cook for me when I pay a housekeeper to do that?"

Gina had been afraid this would happen, but now that it had she didn't have the strength to resist. Instead she put her arms around his neck and curled up against him. His briskly unshaven face was rough against hers and he smelled of whiskey but she didn't care about that as she murmured, "I want to cook for you because drinking on an empty stomach can make you awfully sick."

He pressed her closer. "Would you care if it did, Gina?"

"Of course I would," she murmured against his throat. "After you've eaten you should lie down and sleep, then you'll feel better."

His hand brushed lightly against the side of her breast and she could feel her response deep inside. "If I do will you lie down with me?" he asked.

She wanted to say yes so badly that she had to

clamp her jaws together. Why was she being so stubborn about this? If she wanted to make love with him this much, why didn't she? He was certainly willing. It wasn't as if she was too young to know what she was getting into. At twenty-five she was long past due to lose her virginity. Still she couldn't give in. She had to have some shred of hope that Peter could love her again before she committed herself to him in that way.

She tipped her head and looked up at him. "Is that all you ever think of?" she complained.

He grinned. "Honey, it's almost impossible to think of anything else with you wiggling around on my lap."

His suggestive remark made her intimately aware of his arousal, and her own body responded wildly. Unable to sit still she squirmed against him, and with a low moan his mouth descended on hers, ravishing its willing sweetness. Her arms tightened, holding him close, as heat surged through her, melting her resistance. He wanted her and she wanted him and that's all that mattered: she'd worry about tomorrow when it came.

Peter broke off the kiss and lay his cheek against hers. It was then that Gina realized something was wrong. His skin was cool and damp with a fine film of perspiration. "Peter," she murmured, "are you all right?"

He shook his head almost imperceptibly. "No," he breathed. "My stomach, it's churning. I'm afraid . . ."

He stood up suddenly, dumping her on the sofa beside where they'd been sitting. "Oh sweetheart, I'm sorry . . ."

He stumbled from the room and hurried down the hall toward the bathroom.

Chapter Ten

After summoning Lilly to check on Peter and make sure he was all right, Gina went into the kitchen and, with the aid of Mrs. Webster, heated up the remains of the chicken and rice casserole that had been prepared for lunch. When Peter joined her half an hour later he had shaved, showered and changed into light blue slacks and a matching blue print shirt. The effect was nothing short of devastating to Gina's already short-circuited emotions. With his blue eyes, blond hair and slender but powerful physique he radiated enough sex appeal to start a stampede, but it was his vulnerability that tugged at Gina. The shamed look in his eyes and the lines around his mouth that revealed a still queasy stomach.

The corners of his mouth twitched upward in a tentative smile as he said, "Sorry, I didn't mean to make such a fool of myself back there."

Her heart was doing odd little pit-a-pats that made her voice stumble. "Do—do you feel better now?"

"Yes," he said, watching her. "I always feel better when you're around."

She looked away, hoping he wouldn't notice the effect he was having on her. "Sit down at the table and I'll bring your lunch," she said and began dishing up the chicken and rice. She added an individual molded fruit salad on a bed of lettuce and poured him a cup of coffee.

He eyed the plate of food and pressed his hand against his stomach as he said, "I don't know, honey, I—"

She was standing next to him and squeezed his shoulder gently. "Just try it. You don't need to eat any more than you think your stomach can handle."

He moved his hand to cover hers on his shoulder. "Gina," he said thickly. "Come here. Sit on my lap again."

She was tempted almost beyond endurance but she knew that would be folly. Instead she drew her hand from under his and laughed shakily. "If I did that you wouldn't eat and then you'd be sick again."

"It would be worth it," he murmured.

"Oh, Peter," she groaned and reached out to cradle his head between her breasts. He clasped her around the waist and relaxed against her as she gently stroked his face and hair. "What am I going to do with you?"

He rubbed his cheek against the softness of her and his voice was unsteady as he said, "Touch me, hold me, the way you're doing now. I need your loving tenderness, sweetheart. I became addicted to it seven years ago and these long years without it have been agony."

His actions and his words were tearing her apart. How could she be sensible when her whole being screamed for surrender? Peter had admitted that he wanted her, needed her, was not always able to function without her. Was it really so important that he love her too? Didn't she love enough for both of them?

She leaned down and kissed the top of his clean, shampoo-scented head. "Give me a little time, love. I can't think straight when I'm around you. I never could. You touch me and I melt. We both know that, I was never any good at hiding it, but I can't let you push me into making a decision I'll regret later. I don't think physical attraction, even a passion as strong as ours, is enough on which to base a marriage."

She moved then and turned slightly so she could sit on his lap as he'd asked her to. For long moments they sat clasped in each other's arms, wordlessly glorying in the intimate body contact that they both so greatly desired.

Finally Gina stirred and raised her face to his. "Kiss me, and then eat your lunch before it gets cold."

He grinned and whispered, "Yes ma'am," as his mouth covered hers. It was a sweet and gentle kiss, very much like the first one he had ever given her so many years ago. He cradled her close as his lips caressed hers with a passion that he kept carefully banked and a hunger that he could not contain.

They broke it off reluctantly and Gina stroked his cheek as she whispered, "Oh, Peter, I did love you so."

His gaze held hers. "Did?" he asked.

She closed her eyes to shut out the pleading so visible in his. "I committed myself to you once," she said tightly, "and you decided you didn't want me. I'm not prepared to do that again."

She slid off his lap and strove for lightness. "Come on now and eat your lunch while it's still edible."

He didn't argue and Gina poured herself a cup of

coffee and sat at the table with him as he ate, slowly at first but then with more relish.

They were laughing over something Peter had said that came out backward, an indication that his reflexes were still slowed from all the Scotch, when his mother walked in the kitchen. She gave Gina a chilling glance then focused on Peter. "Peter, my dear," she began in her most effective "concerned mother" voice, "you shouldn't be eating so soon after being ill."

Her gaze shifted to Gina and hardened. "Virginia, I can't imagine what you're thinking of forcing him to eat when you know it will just upset him again."

Gina tensed, prepared to defend herself but Peter was quicker. "I'm feeling much better now, Mother, and Gina most certainly has not forced me to eat."

He reached over and took Gina's hand. "Now, if you'll excuse us we have a lot to talk over and would like to be alone. I'm sure you can find something to do in another part of the house."

For a moment Bertha looked shocked, then her pale face seemed to fall accentuating wrinkles that hadn't been obvious before. Her round fleshy chin trembled and her light blue eyes filled with tears. She aged before their eyes as she sniffed. "I see. Because I've dared to criticize your paramour—"

"My wife, Mother," Peter said between clenched teeth.

Bertha continued as though he hadn't spoken. "I'm being banished to my room like a naughty child. You used to seek my advice, but now you have no use for a mother who loves you."

She paused on a sob and it occurred to Gina that she was witnessing one of Bertha's better performances. It was true what Lilly had said about her mother knowing exactly when to cry, and Bertha was wringing the tears that trickled down her puffy cheeks for all they were worth.

Lilly had been wrong about one thing, though. Peter was not as immune as she had indicated. His hand tightened painfully on Gina's and a muscle twitched in his jaw as his mother continued her tirade. "Fortunately I'm getting old. I won't be around much longer to meddle in your affairs but there's one thing you might consider. If I'm gone who will you go to for comfort the next time this little gold-digging hussy walks out on you?"

"Mother!" Peter roared and jumped up, then leaned heavily on the table for support as a wave of dizziness and nausea swept over him.

Gina pushed back her chair and was on her feet immediately. She put an arm around Peter to steady him and glared at Bertha. "Mrs. Van Housen," she began with icy determination. "If you don't shut up and get out of here right now, I'm personally going to escort you to your room."

The two women locked eyes in silent battle, and it was Bertha who finally turned away and walked out of the kitchen.

Gina eased Peter back in his chair and knelt down beside him. She brushed a lock of hair off his forehead, now damp with perspiration. "Are you all right, darling?" she asked anxiously.

The warmth that flooded his eyes alerted her to her inadvertent use of the endearment, but all he said was, "Just give me a few minutes, I'll be O.K."

He leaned back in the chair and she rose and started cleaning up the dirty dishes. She discovered that she was shaking from the unexpected encounter with Peter's overbearing mother. It was easy to dislike Bertha and yet Gina couldn't altogether blame the older woman. Bertha had been against her son's involvement with a little "commoner," but when she realized that Peter was intent on marriage she'd made an attempt to welcome Gina into the family only to have to stand by later and watch her son's anguish when his bride proved, at least to the eyes of the family, to be an unfaithful money-grabber. Gina knew she would have felt the same had it been her son who was involved.

She sighed. It was all such a tangled web and they couldn't go on this way. The whole situation was getting out of control and had to be resolved, now. Either she must live with Peter who desired her but did not love her in a marriage that would probably not endure once the passion had been satisfied, or she must finally make him understand that she wanted the marriage terminated immediately.

She glanced anxiously over at him. He was slumped in his chair and looked pale and exhausted. He was temporarily vulnerable now, but by tomorrow he'd be strong and invincible again. Peter was a fighter, a leader, a man sufficient unto himself, and she suspected that he wasn't above using some of the tricks his mother found so valuable in getting her own way.

Is that what he was doing to her now? Gina wondered. Had she been set up? Was his drinking a deliberate ploy to gain her sympathy and make her even more susceptible to him? She shook her head. No, that was unlikely. There was no doubt but that the drinking had made him violently ill, and she couldn't believe that he'd deliberately bring that on himself. He couldn't want her that badly! It was more likely that it had started as a temper tantrum because she'd dared to resist him and then had gotten out of hand.

Peter looked up and caught her watching him, then frowned when he saw what she was doing. "Gina, you don't have to wash dishes. We have a housekeeper for that."

She grinned. "I know. Guess I'm just a compulsive tidier, but I can't see any reason to leave these for Mrs. Webster when I'm standing around doing nothing. Besides, it's a joy to work in this kitchen, it's so clean and shiny and well-organized."

"It's your kitchen, sweetheart," he said softly, "You can do anything in it you want to. But I can think of a much more interesting diversion than washing dirty dishes." He winked suggestively.

"Peter Van Housen!" Gina laughed. "You have a one-track mind. Besides," she teased, "didn't anyone ever tell you that the diversion you have in mind is better performed in the bedroom with the door shut?"

"I've been trying for weeks to get you behind the closed door of a bedroom," he said tersely, all humor gone. "I'm at the point where I'll take it anywhere I can get it."

Gina sobered quickly and realized she'd asked for that. It had not only been a stupid way to tease him, it had also been cruel. He wasn't feeling well enough for bright repartee at the moment.

She dried her hands and went over to stand beside him. "I'm sorry, Peter," she apologized, "that was a thoughtless thing to say. You still look pretty rocky. I really do think you should go upstairs and take a nap."

He looked up at her. "I don't suppose it will do any good to ask you to take a nap with me?"

She shook her head. "No."

He let out his breath and pushed himself off the chair. He stood but reached out to hold onto Gina as the dizziness returned. "Sorry," he muttered, "but I'm afraid you're going to have to help me upstairs."

She put her arm around his waist and gave him the support he needed to negotiate the long hall between the library and the living room, past the family room, Peter's office and a bathroom and up the wide rustic stairway at the end.

At the top of the stairs Gina paused and Peter looked at her quizzically until he remembered. "That's right, you haven't been up here before, have you? I never did give you the grand tour of the house."

He had his arm around her shoulders and hers was around his waist. The feel of his tall sturdy body pressing hip to hip and thigh to thigh with hers was rapidly melting her bones and she knew if they stood together like that much longer, she'd go to bed with him whether he asked her again or not.

"I'll tour your house another time," she said crisply. "For now just tell me where your bedroom is."

He grinned. "Yes ma'am, happy to oblige," he said as he hugged her closer to him and turned to the left. "It's the first door down the hall."

He didn't let loose of her as they walked through the door, and her eyes widened as she surveyed the beautifully decorated room. It was huge, big enough for two rooms, with a fireplace at one end that was a continuation of the stone fireplace in the rooms directly below. The outside wall was a replica of the glass wall in the living room and it also opened onto a redwood deck. The sheer eggshell curtains that covered the glass did little to obstruct the sweeping view of the ocean, only this time she could see even further because of the higher vantage point.

The room was furnished in dark reddish-brown

cherry wood; the focal piece was a king-size bed covered with a quilted puff satin spread in a swirl design ranging from navy to sky blue with tiny streaks of scarlet and cream for accent. Several tables and chests, including a very feminine dressing table with a lighted mirror, were grouped around the bed, and at the other end of the room a blue velvet sofa and two upholstered chairs, one scarlet and one cream, faced the fireplace.

Gina was entranced. It was the most luxurious bedroom she'd ever seen. She felt like Alice in Wonderland. "Oh Peter," she breathed, "it's so—so right! I've never seen anything so elegant."

He lowered his head and kissed her cheek. "I'm glad you like it. I had it decorated for you."

"For me?" She felt her resistance weakening. It would be sheer heaven to share this room with Peter, to lie curled in his arms at night and listen to the surf pounding against the shore. To waken in the morning to sunlight streaming through the glass and breakfast for two on the deck.

She mentally shook herself and pulled abruptly away from him. "Peter," she said hotly. "Don't you ever give up? Did you honestly believe that if you couldn't seduce me with sex you could buy me with all this?"

She swept her arms to indicate not only the room but the whole house. "You really believe you can get anything you want with money, don't you?"

He looked surprised by her sudden outburst and his voice was cool when he responded. "I know I can, but with you I shouldn't have to. You're my wife, I'm entitled to have you in my bed and I've about reached the end of my patience with this outraged virgin act of yours."

Gina gasped and he grabbed her by the shoulders and shook her as anger replaced the surprise on his face. "You're driving me out of my mind. You touch me, caress me, allow me enticing liberties and then act offended when I want more. You respond to my lovemaking until I'm half crazy with need, then pull away and insist that I stop. Stop! Just turn it off like a light switch! My God, Gina, don't you know what that does to a man?"

His fingers dug into her flesh until she cried out with pain, but he was too enraged now to hear her. He jerked her against him and held her with one arm around her waist while his other hand gripped the back of her head so she couldn't move it as his mouth swooped down and took hers prisoner. Gone was the patient gentleness; it had been replaced by a much more violent emotion, out of control and dangerous.

Gina struggled ineffectually as his mouth ground into hers, lustful and hurting. For the first time she was afraid of Peter. His hold on her was bruising and her breath came in short painful sobs as she tried desperately to move her head away from the pressure that was causing her teeth to rip the soft flesh on the underside of her lips.

When he finally lifted his head she drew breath into her lungs in shuddering gulps. He looked at her with a stunned expression, as though he had just realized that he'd been hurting her. She seized the moment to push him hard, and as she did, his hold loosened and she wrenched herself out of his grasp. She stood facing him, panting with exertion and fear, and her voice was loud and tinged with hysteria as she said, "You're never to blame for anything, are you? You won't leave me alone. You seduce me with your expert lovemaking and when I respond it's *my* fault.

I've told you in every way I know how that I don't want your kisses and embraces but you continue to force them on me and then accuse *me* of being a tease. Now you've decided to play rough because I've had the audacity to refuse to become your legal prostitute!"

She turned and rushed from the room. When Peter called her name she started to run, but she'd forgotten about the sharp turn at the top of the stairway and was going too fast to maneuver it successfully. Her foot slipped and she plunged, screaming with surprise and terror, down the long flight of wide, carpeted stairs!

It seemed to Gina that it took forever for her tortured body to tumble from one step to another to another . . . like a time warp where all movement is slowed. She heard someone shouting, and a scream that could have been coming from her, although she wasn't conscious of making a sound except for the thump, thump, thump as she fell further and further . . .

Then as suddenly as it began, it stopped. Pain wracked every inch of her but she was finally still. She was vaguely aware of footsteps and voices coming from all directions, and when she forced her eyes to open she saw Peter kneeling beside her, his face white and stricken. She could see his lips moving but there was so much confusion that she couldn't understand what he was saying. She closed her eyes again because it was too much of an effort to keep them open.

Later, whether seconds, minutes or hours she couldn't tell, she felt herself floating. She moved her head against something solid and it fitted into the hollow of a shoulder, Peter's shoulder. He was carrying her back up the stairs. Then slowly, carefully, he lowered her onto a cloud, soft and smooth and fragrant, and she snuggled gratefully into it and blotted out the pain and the noise.

"Gina! Gina, open your eyes and look at me!" The command was sharp and insistent and she huddled deeper into the pillow trying to shut it out. She ached everywhere and all she wanted was the luxury of oblivion.

"Gina!" Now a hand was shaking her gently. Whoever it was wasn't going to give up, and she struggled out of the fuzzy darkness and opened her eyes. She was lying on a bed and a man was sitting beside her, a stranger with sandy hair thinning on top and a solemn expression.

"Who—who are you," she whispered through dry lips.

The man looked relieved and smiled. "I'm Dr. Bowmer. Can you tell me who you are?"

"Virginia Lea Brown," she confessed slowly.

"Good," said the doctor. "Now tell me what day today is."

She looked at him with disbelief. "Did you wake me just to ask me that?" she grumbled then answered, "It's Tuesday."

"Right!" The doctor beamed, as pleased as if she had recited Einstein's theory of relativity backward. "Now just one more question. What's your husband's name?"

"I don't have a husband."

Dr. Bowmer frowned. "Then can you tell me who you were with just before you fell?"

"Fell?" For a minute she didn't know what he was talking about, then it all came back. "Oh, you mean Peter. Well yes, I guess you could say that Peter is my husband. His name is Peter Van Housen but you must know that. I assume he brought you here."

She didn't feel like answering his stupid questions and wished he'd leave and let her sleep.

He seemed inordinately happy with her last answer and took her wrist between his thumb and fingers. "That's a girl," he said happily. "You'll be okay. You've got a sprained ankle and some nasty bruises but I doubt that you have a concussion, although you'll probably have a king-size headache for a day or two. You're a lucky young woman, you know."

Gina grimaced. "Your definition of luck is obscene, doctor," she groaned.

He chuckled. "You'll feel better tomorrow." He picked up a hypodermic syringe from the bedside table and adjusted it. "I'll give you an injection to dull the pain and help you sleep. Have Peter bring you in to the hospital at Fort Bragg tomorrow and we'll take some X-rays but I'm sure nothing's broken. You'll have to stay off that foot for a while."

She felt the prick of the needle and a few minutes later she was asleep.

When she woke again it was dark except for the light of the full moon that stole softly into the room through the glass wall. She was sore all over but the pain seemed concentrated in her right foot and her head. Her gaze wandered around and she recognized her whereabouts as Peter's bedroom, but she wasn't sure how she'd gotten there. Her memory was hazy after that first terrifying sensation of falling.

She closed her eyes, trying to shut out the throbbing in her head, but when she shifted to find a more comfortable position needles of agony shot up her leg from the ankle to the knee and she uttered a sharp cry that ended in a moan. A rustle from the other end of the room alerted her to the fact that she was not alone, and it was Peter's voice that spoke as he hurried toward the bed. "Gina, darling, what's the matter?"

He loomed above her, a shadowy figure that she had trouble focusing her eyes on until he lowered himself to sit on the edge of the wide bed beside her. He took her hand and raised it to his lips, then pressed it against his cheek and held it there. "Are you in pain?" he asked, his voice full of concern.

"Yes," she said. "My ankle . . . and my head."

He put his fingers on her forehead and stroked gently. "The doctor bandaged your ankle, it should feel better tomorrow, but he left some pills to make you more comfortable."

He reached over and flipped a switch that lit a dim nightlight in the base of the crystal lamp which stood on the table by the bed. It cast a soft glow that illuminated without hurting her eyes. She was astonished to find that she was wearing a man's navy blue silk pajama coat and nothing else.

She looked at Peter and was troubled by what she saw. He looked almost as bad as she felt. His hair, usually so carefully groomed, was tousled, his clothes were rumpled and his eyes were red-rimmed and haunted. His skin was a pasty gray and he looked even sicker than he had earlier in the day.

She reached out her hand and touched his lips with her fingers. He kissed them and she moved upward to gently stroke the purple circles under his eyes. He flinched, almost as though she had struck him, and captured her hand in his as he muttered thickly, "Gina, oh God, how can you be so sweet after what I did to you?"

Her brow wrinkled in thought as she tried to

remember. "Did to me?" she said. "What do you mean?"

He looked at her for a moment, then squeezed her hand and laid it on her chest. "Never mind," he said as he picked up a small prescription jar from the table. "We'll talk tomorrow."

He shook a couple of pills from the jar and poured ice water from a covered pitcher into a glass and added a flexible straw. "Here," he said and handed her the tablets. "Take these. No need to sit up, just sip water through this."

He held the glass down and guided the straw to her mouth while she swallowed the pills, then set it back on the tray with the pitcher and turned off the night light leaving the room in darkness once more.

He leaned over and kissed her lightly on the lips. "Go back to sleep, I'll be right here beside you."

He sat there holding her hand until she was no longer aware of him.

The next time Gina woke it was daylight, a gray foggy daylight but her watch, which had miraculously escaped the fall unbroken, told her it was mid-morning. She moved cautiously and discovered she could do so with reasonable ease, all except for her right ankle. It had to be maneuvered carefully.

She rolled over and was startled to see Peter lying in the bed beside her; his chest above the covering sheet was bare. He was on his side facing her, his eyes closed and his body sprawled in a relaxed position, his face peaceful in sleep. His blond hair spilled over his brow and his long thick brown lashes lay against the dark hollows under his eyes.

A warm tenderness swept through her. He looked so different when he slept. There was no trace of the hard driving businessman or the cynical lover who looked on seduction as a game. This Peter was boyish, trusting, defenseless. He had chosen to spend the night here with her knowing that by letting down his guard he was putting himself at her mercy. If she should decide to extract revenge for his behavior yesterday she could make life miserable for him.

She reached out and very softly cupped his cheek with her hand. It was smooth against her palm and she remembered that he had shaved late the day before. With her thumb she stroked the side of his neck and his jaw as her fingertips caressed one closed eyelid.

It didn't stay closed long but opened to uncover sea-blue eyes that looked directly into her deep violet ones. He didn't blink or smile and his voice was husky as he said, "For seven years I've dreamed of waking up to find you in bed beside me."

He moved closer and raised up so he could kiss her. His lips on hers were warm and gentle as his arm slid under her neck, careful not to jar her head. She returned his kiss and let her hands wander over his nude shoulders. His muscles rippled under her touch and she marveled that a man as slender as Peter could be so strong.

He lifted his head to look at her and she caught her breath at the torment she saw on his face. "Gina," he said hoarsely, then swallowed and started again. "Oh darling, I'm so sorry."

He buried his face in her shoulder and her arms slid around him. She knew he was blaming himself for her fall and she hurried to reassure him. "It wasn't your fault, Peter, it was an accident."

He moved away from her and propped himself up with his elbow. "Don't delude yourself, Gina," he said harshly. "If I hadn't lost control and scared you half to death you wouldn't have run away from me in such a panic and stumbled on that turn. When I heard you scream and saw you lying in a heap at the bottom of the stairs I . . ."

He bit his lower lip and closed his eyes, but his grim features mirrored his silent battle not to give way to the emotions that were tearing at him. Gina put her arms up and pulled him back down to her, cradling his head between her soft white breasts. He was lying fully against her now and she was relieved to feel the crisp silk of his pajama bottoms. She wasn't sure she could have tempered her reaction if he'd been totally unclothed!

She brushed the disheveled hair off his cheek. "Don't blame yourself, sweetheart, I wasn't afraid of you. I—I think I was afraid of myself."

His mouth caressed her breast and his hand stroked her bare thigh. "You don't understand. I tricked you into coming up here. My dizziness wasn't that bad, I didn't need help to get upstairs. I wanted you to come with me and I didn't know how else to get you to do it."

There was a smile in her voice as she said, "I know, or at least I suspected as much, but I went with you anyway. I'm not as naïve as you give me credit for."

Peter looked up at her, then rolled away and sat up cross-legged on the bed. "If that's true then why are you tormenting us this way?" he asked tersely. "If you want me, then why won't you stay with me? What do you hope to gain by holding out?"

Gina knew he was right, she was being inconsistent. Telling herself she didn't want him to make love to her when her whole body screamed for his possession.

She met his accusing gaze that stabbed through her with the thrust of a blade. "You're oversimplifying it," she said, wondering if she could make him understand. "I want more out of marriage than just good sex. I want a husband who will love me, trust me, cherish me, and in return I'll give him children and a lifetime of loving. I'll never get any of those things from you, Peter. You're too suspicious and willing to believe the worst of me. I could never trust you not to walk out on me again, and nobody does that to me twice."

His eyes blazed with anger and he got off the bed and stood facing her. "The best way to assure my fidelity," he said in a voice like chipped ice, "is to never again give me as good a reason to walk out as you did last time."

He picked up his clothes and stalked out of the room.

Chapter Eleven

Later that day when Gina could sit up without her head pounding Peter drove her to the hospital. They chatted politely about nothing of consequence all the way to Fort Bragg and at the hospital, after a series of X-rays, Gina was told that there was nothing broken and that her ankle, although sore, would heal quickly if she stayed off it as much as possible.

On the way back Gina insisted that she was perfectly capable of taking care of herself at her apartment but Peter outvoted her. They stopped in Mendocino only long enough to pack some clothes for her and arrange for Peg Harvey to run the gallery for a few days, then returned to Peter's home. Gina knew she should have insisted on staying in Mendocino, but her head hurt, she couldn't put any weight on her ankle, and besides it was impossible to argue with Peter; he refused to listen.

As they drove down the scenic highway Gina sank back wearily in the plush seat of the Jaguar and sighed. At least she wouldn't have to contend with the rest of Peter's family. Hans, Bertha, Lilly and the two children had left for San Francisco shortly after Peter stormed out of the bedroom that morning. She was sorry she hadn't had a chance to visit with Johnny and Sonja before they took off, but Peter had been adamant about not letting any of them disturb her.

Only Lilly braved her brother's wrath and forced her way into the bedroom to say good-bye. She sat by the side of the bed and took Gina's hand as she said, "You gave us an awful scare, you know. You and Peter had better settle your differences soon before one or both of you are damaged beyond repair."

She leaned over and kissed Gina on the cheek. "Don't be too hard on my little brother, honey. He's stubborn, spoiled and has a temper like a buzz saw, but he loves you to distraction."

Gina squeezed the hand that held hers. "Oh Lilly, if only that were true . . ."

"It is true, Gina, believe me. I'm older than you and wiser than Peter, I can see what each of you is too proud to admit. Stay with him, you won't be sorry. Besides, I like having you for a sister-in-law."

Gina was nearly asleep when they arrived at the house, and Peter carried her upstairs and told Mrs. Webster to put her to bed. She slept until Mrs. Webster brought her dinner tray. Later Peter came in to ask how she was feeling, select an assortment of clean clothes and tell her that he would be sleeping in the room down the hall. He showed her how to use the intercom system to call Mrs. Webster should she need help during the night then bent to brush his lips across hers in a hurried good night kiss and left.

It was only then that Gina realized how much she'd been looking forward to sharing the oversized bed with him again. She grimaced with disgust. She so badly wanted to believe as Lilly did that he loved her but she knew she was only deluding herself. Peter had made it plain, not once but several times, that the love he once felt for her was dead and he had no intention of resurrecting it.

Unfortunately she wasn't able to turn off her feelings for Peter that easily. She loved him, she'd always love him, she wasn't sure she could live without him, but she knew she couldn't live with him never knowing when he might fall in love with someone else and want out. The sooner she got away from him the better.

The next morning after Mrs. Webster had brought her breakfast and helped her dress, Peter carried her downstairs to the library where she chose a current novel and stretched out on the couch to read while he worked in his office. He joined her for lunch on the deck and afterward settled her in the same lounge chair that they had both shared two days before. He tucked her in with a cashmere lap robe to protect her against the cool ocean breeze, gave her a brotherly peck on the cheek and returned to his office.

He was the perfect nurse, cool, efficient and cheerful but uninvolved on a personal level. Gina blinked back tears as she remembered sharing this lounger with Peter, the sweetness of their early caresses and later the fire of their shared passion. If only they hadn't been interrupted. She had been past the point of resistance; she would have given herself to him gladly and with love. At least then she would have known exactly how he felt about her, one way or the other, and could have planned her future accordingly.

That evening they had dinner in the dining room.

Afterward Peter carried her back up to his bedroom and again left her with a light goodnight kiss and walked down the hall to another bed.

The following day was more of the same, and by evening Gina was a bundle of screaming nerve ends. The inactivity was bad enough, but Peter's cheerful brotherly attitude was driving her right up the wall. She had to get out of there! She had a lot of bruises but her head no longer hurt and she was able to walk with a limp but at least she could get around.

They had dinner in the family room in front of a cheerful fire in the rustic stone fireplace, sitting together on the couch and eating from lap trays. Gina was so aware of Peter's nearness that she hardly tasted the spaghetti with white clam sauce, the tossed fresh spinach and bacon salad, hot buttered french bread and wine.

When they had finished eating Peter carried their trays to the kitchen and brought back a silver coffee service. Gina's hand shook with nervousness as she poured the coffee. She'd made up her mind to confront Peter about leaving and couldn't put it off any longer.

She handed him a cup but left hers sitting on the table as she said, "I—I'm getting around quite well now, Peter, and I'm anxious to get back to the shop."

He looked at her and smiled. "It's still too early, give it a few more days. If you're worried about your business I can have one of our people at the gallery in San Francisco come up for a week or so and take over."

She shook her head. "No, you don't understand. I can't stand this inactivity. I need to get back to work. I want to go home."

She knew by his expression that he wasn't going to

agree. The smile was gone, the shuttered look back on his face. "You are home, Gina," he said as he set his cup beside hers.

She clutched her hands together in her lap to still their trembling. "No, Peter," she said, "I'm not. I appreciate your wanting to share this beautiful place with me but I can't stay here. I'm going back to Mendocino."

He looked at her without expression and his voice was cold. "You don't have any intention of trying to make this marriage work, do you." It wasn't a question but a statement.

She looked away, unable to hold his unwavering gaze. "No, I don't," she said in a voice that quivered with emotion. "Our marriage died seven years ago, let it rest in peace."

"I'd be happy to," he said grimly, "but unfortunately it's not that simple. I've found no peace in these intervening years and I don't think you have either. What do you want from me, Gina? It seems to me that if I'm willing to forgive and try to forget you certainly should be."

There it was again, his absolute certainty that she had lied, cheated and tricked him into marriage. He was implacable on that issue; she was the sinner and he had been sinned against. It was true, he had been sinned against, but not by her!

She closed her eyes against the pain and forced her voice to remain steady as she said, "Why do you refuse to understand, Peter? I've told you so often. When I was eighteen I gave you all that I had to give—my love. I figuratively laid my heart at your feet and you trampled on it. When you walked out on me without trying to understand my side of the story I wanted to die."

Peter caught his breath but she continued. "No please, don't interrupt. I waited for you to come back, even if it was to ask for an annulment, but you sent your lawyer instead with threats of retribution if I tried to get any money from you." She grimaced. "That's all the breakup of our brief marriage meant to you, the amount of money it would cost to get rid of me."

"No, Gina—" Peter gasped, but she wasn't listening.

"The newspaper columnists had a field day. For weeks there was public speculation over why the most eligible bachelor in San Francisco had walked out on his bride only hours after the wedding. The reporters hounded me constantly. I couldn't even go out of the house without being accosted by photographers and newspeople."

She shuddered. "I was left completely at their mercy and I had no idea how to handle it. I was both frightened and mortified, and not once did a member of the Van Housen family try to protect me. You disappeared and your parents and brothers were unavailable in their impenetrable mansion in the Sea Cliff district. My family and I were thrown to that pack of wolves and left to survive as best we could."

She looked squarely at Peter then and let the hostility blaze from her eyes. "We survived by uprooting our lives and moving three thousand miles across the country and now you have the gall to accuse *me* of running away! *You* ran out when I needed you, Peter, and I managed to put my life back together and live without you. Now all I want from you is the same thing I've asked you for over and over, my freedom. I don't want your house, or your money, or your influence, I just want to have this farce of a marriage dissolved so I can get on with my life."

She raised her head to look at him and was surprised to find a grimace of such utter desolation on his face that she unwittingly uttered a little cry and held out her hand, but before she could touch him the cold, hard look had returned and she decided she'd only imagined the other. She was sure of it a few seconds later when he got up and walked to the fireplace where he stood with his back to her looking into the flames.

He jammed his hands into the pockets of his gray flannel slacks. "All right, Gina," he said with icy deliberation. "I'll give you your freedom."

She gasped, but it sounded more like a sob. Before she could say anything, however, he continued, "I'll agree to a dissolution on one condition, that you spend one night making love with me."

She stared at his back, stunned. It wasn't possible that she'd heard what she thought she had. Even Peter wouldn't make a demand like that!

But she knew that he would. If he wanted something badly enough Peter Van Housen would use any means to get it, and he knew her weakness for him. Well, this time he had gone too far. She had no intentions of submitting to blackmail!

She stood and was appalled to find that her knees were shaking. "Well thanks but no thanks," she said with what she hoped was the proper amount of sarcasm. "If you'll excuse me, I'll go pack."

She started to limp toward the door but he swung around and caught her, pulling her roughly into his arms. "*Now* Gina!" he muttered as his lips pressed tingling little kisses from her temple to her ear.

"Tonight! I've been behaving like an inexperienced teenager letting you torment me, but no more. You've run out of time, love, and now you're going to pay up."

He nuzzled the sensitive hollow at the side of her throat and set her pulse to pounding.

She tried to pull away but his arms tightened and his hand found its way under her pull-over knit blouse and cupped one of her lace-covered breasts. A wave of heat surged through her leaving a thin film of moisture on her skin and she knew if she didn't do something quickly she'd be lost. She struggled but was no match for his strength.

Maybe she could reason with him. She stopped fighting and he unfastened her bra and gently massaged her nipple, bringing it to a throbbing peak. "Peter," she begged. "Don't. Oh please don't do this to me! Surely you don't intend to force me when you know I'm unwilling!"

Somehow, without her realizing it, he had managed to unfasten the button on her white slacks and his hand dipped under the waistband and stroked the bare small of her back. "I wouldn't dream of forcing you," he murmured against her ear. "It won't be necessary. You want this almost as much as I do. Even as you say you're unwilling, you respond to me, you always have."

His hand moved lower and he made little circular motions against the swell of her buttocks. He was right! She arched against him without ever willing it. Her traitorous body was on fire with desire for him and when he swung her into his arms and headed for the stairway she clasped her arms around his neck and buried her flaming face in his shoulder.

In the beautiful blue master bedroom he stood her

beside the huge bed and started to remove her blouse. With a last effort at self-preservation she folded her arms across her chest and shook her head from side to side. "No, no, please no."

He didn't argue but kissed her tenderly and started removing her slacks instead. She gave in then and let him undress her. He lowered her to the bed, then undressed himself and slid in beside her. She shivered with need as he drew her naked body against his own and sought her moist trembling lips.

Gina made one last effort to resist by clenching her teeth and refusing to return the kiss. She could feel the tightly leashed tension in him as he moved against her and moaned, "Don't fight me, sweetheart. I don't want to be rough, but I'm rapidly losing control. Please Gina, let me love you."

She slid her arms around him then and opened her mouth to his plundering tongue as they both ignited in flame. He seemed to know exactly where to touch and caress her to bring her to the edge of madness and she wasn't prepared for the sharp searing pain that accompanied his total possession. She stiffened and for a moment neither of them moved as they lay suspended on the brink of ecstasy.

Gina opened her eyes and saw Peter's face above her, frozen with surprise. For a second she was afraid he was going to withdraw and her arms tightened around him as his voice, raw with anguish, sounded against her ear. "Oh my lovely Gina!"

It was a cry of pain, not of the flesh but of the spirit. Then with infinite tenderness he began once more the rhythm of passion, bringing her slowly, carefully, to the radiant joy of shared release that bonded them together and made them one.

Afterward he held her, gentled her, until her

breathing stabilized and she returned slowly to the real world. Then he rolled away from her and sat on the side of the bed with his back to her, his shoulders slumped and his hands hanging loosely between his knees. It was then that she knew she had been wrong. Their union hadn't bonded them together, but had wrenched them even further apart. Peter knew now beyond any doubt that she had never made love with Mel Calicutt or any other man, but the knowledge had come too late. It no longer made any difference to him. The wonder had all been on her part: for him the experience had been a disappointment.

She was still too vulnerable to control her emotions and tears welled in her eyes and ran down her face as she put out her hand and touched his bare hip. "Peter?" she whispered.

He didn't turn to look at her and his voice was flat as he said, "I didn't mean to hurt you, Gina. I—I didn't know . . . I should have stopped but I couldn't . . . I just couldn't."

He rubbed his hands over his face then stood and began dressing quickly. Gina wanted to tell him that the pain in her body had been minor, but the pain in her soul was so great that all she could do was sob and bury her face in her pillow.

She felt his hand stroking her hair. "I'm sorry. I can't possibly tell you how sorry," he said in that wooden tone and walked out of the room, closing the door softly behind him. A few minutes later she heard the powerful engine of the Jaguar roar to life and tear off into the night.

Gina shuddered convulsively and chastised herself for being such a baby. *Grown up women don't cry,* she told herself fiercely as she sat up and swung her feet to the floor. *Grown women meet life head on and take their lumps.* She reached for a tissue and blew her nose. *The only trouble is you can get an awfully lumpy head that way!* She stood and started toward the bathroom.

The needles of hot pulsating water from the shower stung her creamy skin, but had the desired effect of making her feel alive again and ready to fight the depression that had threatened to overwhelm her. She'd let Peter do that to her once and it had taken her years to feel like a woman again. This time she'd suspected that he would walk out once he'd had his fill of her but she hadn't expected it to come so soon. What had gone wrong? She'd achieved a mind-blowing ecstasy, why hadn't he?

Gina had been prepared for the anguish Peter's departure would bring. She'd been through that before, but what she hadn't expected was the blow it had been to her ego. She'd never doubted but that he would find as much fulfillment in their love-making as she would and it was shattering to her very womanhood to know that she was so lacking in ability to please him.

Maybe if she'd been more experienced; if she hadn't clung to her virginity all these years; if she'd gone to bed with some of the men who had been so anxious to take her, then she would have learned the more sophisticated ways to make the act memorable.

She turned off the water and reached for a soft fluffy towel. "Stop it, Gina!" she said aloud as she dried herself vigorously. She hadn't been "saving" her virginity, she was simply incapable of engaging in indiscriminate love affairs and if that made her too inexpert for Peter's taste, then so be it.

She wasn't going to wallow in self-pity. She had a business to run. It wouldn't take the place of the husband and children she wanted but it was a living, a challenge, and hopefully a device to keep her sane.

A glance at her wristwatch told her that it was ten o'clock but she knew better than to try to sleep. It was going to be a long night and she wasn't going to spend it tossing and turning in bed, tearing herself apart thinking of Peter. She dressed in blue jeans and a pink velour long-sleeved blouse to ward off the damp night chill and used the blow dryer to style and dry her hair.

She was just finishing with her hair when the doorbell rang. *Who on earth could that be at this hour?* she thought as she limped out of her room and down the stairs. She knew the door would be answered by one of the Websters but she felt a shiver of apprehension. It couldn't be Peter; he had his own key and wouldn't ring for admittance. But who else would come to this secluded place at such a late hour?

She heard Bud Webster's voice as she hurried down the hall and when she got to the entryway she saw that he was speaking to someone through the closed oak door, reluctant to open it at this hour. "Who is it, Mr. Webster?" she asked.

"It's a lady, ma'am, says her name is Twyla Sisson."

"Twyla!" Gina cried as she rushed to the door and unlocked it. "Twyla," she said again as she hugged the large woman who stepped through the open doorway.

Twyla was dressed in black slacks and a matching fleece-lined parka and she returned Gina's hug as she said, "Peter called and asked me to come. He said you needed me. What has that chauvinist pig done to you now?"

Gina laughed because it was either that or cry and she was determined not to shed any more tears. "Oh Twyla, what did I ever do to deserve a friend like you? Come in. Here, let me take your jacket."

Twyla shrugged out of her parka and handed it to Gina. Underneath she wore a red- and gray-striped sweater and she rubbed at her arms as she said, "It's cold out there. The breeze is coming directly off the ocean."

She walked into the living room while Gina hung her jacket in the coat closet and told Mr. Webster that she wouldn't need either him or his wife anymore that evening. When Gina joined Twyla her friend was standing in the middle of the room gazing around with undisguised appreciation. "I've never seen such a beautiful home," she said in a voice filled with admiration. "It belongs to Peter I assume."

Gina nodded her affirmative answer. "I'll take you on a tour of the place later, but now come with me to the family room and I'll fix us both a drink."

Twyla stirred up the dying embers of the fireplace and added a log while Gina poured brandy into two crystal snifters. They sat on the couch with their feet tucked under them and sipped the warm smooth drink for a few minutes before Twyla opened the conversation. "Is Peter here?"

Gina shook her head. "No, he left about half an hour ago."

"Did you two quarrel?"

"Not at all." Gina's voice was bitter. "Tonight he finally melted the last of my resistance and took me to bed. When it was over he got up, dressed, apologized and left."

Twyla's brown eyes widened. "Just like that?"

"Just like that," confirmed Gina. "He was so disappointed by my performance that he didn't even pretend that he'd enjoyed it, he just said he was sorry and walked out."

Her voice broke but she forced herself to go on.

"I—I've been thinking and I've come to the conclusion that this was all part of his revenge for my supposed deception. I believe he planned to seduce me and then deliberately let me know how little I meant to him by doing just what he did."

I must have thrown him a curve when he found out I was still a virgin, she thought with a touch of vengeful satisfaction. *That's probably why he apologized.*

She put her hands over her eyes and stiffened against the pain that washed over her. "Well, I hope he's happy now because his little scheme worked." She curled up in a ball and buried her face in her knees.

Twyla muttered a curse that questioned Peter's parentage then seemed somewhat doubtful of her diagnosis. "Are you sure, Gina?" she asked. "Maybe you misunderstood his actions. He sounded a little frantic with concern when he called me. He didn't tell me what was wrong, only that you needed me and to please come right away. I dropped everything and came running."

Gina looked at her friend and appreciation vied with the tears that shimmered in her eyes. "And I thought you were mad at me," she murmured.

"I was," Twyla shrugged, "but I got over it. In case you're still interested I called Stewart the other day and invited him over for pan-fried chicken and country gravy. We talked and, well, it's going to take him a while to get over you but if I keep plying him with home cooking it might speed up the healing process and, who knows, we may get together yet."

Gina wasn't fooled by her friend's levity and she put her hand on Twyla's arm. "Oh Twyla," she said huskily. "I hope so."

Twyla smiled and patted the hand on her arm. "I'm

sure of it," she said, "but I didn't come here to talk about my love life. It's yours I'm concerned about. Now come on, give."

Gina cleared her throat and blinked away the tears. "I was crying when Peter left. He probably had an attack of conscience and decided he'd better see to it that I was taken care of."

She tipped the snifter to her lips and swallowed the last of the brandy. "Take me home, Twyla."

Twyla nodded and stood. "Come on, I'll help you get your things together."

Chapter Twelve

The noonday sun shone brightly on the churning ocean as the biting wind slammed huge blue-green waves topped with white foam against the rocky Mendocino coast line. Gina, wearing a heather wool pleated skirt and a bulky gray sweater buttoned up against the chill of the strong breeze, stood on top of the cliff bracing herself into the gusts and watching the swirling ever-changing sea. She'd taken advantage of her lunch break to get away from the shop, her apartment, the small village that held so many memories and walk the short distance to the ocean.

It had been two days since that disastrous night with Peter and she'd heard nothing from him. Not that she'd really expected to, but that didn't make the yearning any less painful. She'd managed to fill her days with work but the nights were unrelenting torture. If it hadn't been for Twyla she didn't know how she would have survived.

On the drive back to Mendocino from Peter's home she'd filled Twyla in on the events leading up to his seduction and then abandonment of her. Twyla, in her own colorful language that at times seared even Gina's ears, denounced Peter in particular and all men in general as ungrateful, immoral and fatherless.

Later, though, during the past two nights when she'd just happened to drop by to gossip and, incidentally, keep Gina from going insane with loneliness and regret, she'd been less sure of Peter's motives. "It's just not Peter's style, honey," she'd said in a puzzled tone. "It's too crude. I'm positive he'd never be less than a gentleman in an intimate relationship with a woman. Are you sure you've told me everything?"

Of course Gina hadn't told her friend "everything." She could never discuss the details of their lovemaking with anyone, but all the pertinent facts were there. Peter had seduced her, made love to her, and then walked out on her.

A strong gust of wind tossed breaking waves high on the jagged face of the cliff and rocked Gina with its chilling force. She pulled her sweater tighter and turned to walk back toward town. If she didn't hurry she would overstay her break and today had been a busy one. This was the Labor Day weekend, the last big tourist influx before the schools started in California. After Monday the summer season would be over and fall was already blowing in on the tides.

Gina's black hair was tousled and her cheeks were pink from the nippy breeze as she stepped into the gallery and closed the door behind her. To her left two middle-aged women were standing in front of a glass display case arguing with Peg Harvey over the price of a sleek ceramic cat, and Gina walked toward them on her way to her office to hang up her sweater.

She smiled at Peg as she started to pass, but Peg held up a hand to stop her. "Gina," she said, "you have a visitor."

Gina turned in the direction of Peg's glance and froze. Not four steps behind her stood Peter Van Housen.

He was wearing brown corduroy jeans and a tan windbreaker and his wheat-colored hair was ruffled from the breeze, but he did not look boyish. If anything he'd aged in the two days since she'd seen him. He'd looked ill then and he still did, but there was something else. The slump of his shoulders, his stance, were more like that of an old man worn down by defeat than the cocky attitude he'd always maintained.

His face was clean-shaven and she could smell the scent of his musky lotion, but the lines around his mouth had deepened and his eyes had a bruised look about them. He didn't resemble a man who recently tasted the sweetness of revenge.

He took a step forward and for a moment she thought he was going to take her in his arms. Surely the magnetism between them was too strong to be one-sided, but again she was wrong. He thrust his hands into the pockets of his windbreaker and said, "I want to talk to you, Gina."

Talk to me? Gina thought incredulously. *Oh yes, by all means let's talk. Let's be civilized about this and flay each other with words instead of whips. Words don't leave a mark on the body for all to see, they just shrivel the soul.*

She swallowed and hoped she could speak. "Of course. What is it you want?" It came out pretty well considering that her whole body was quivering.

He frowned. "Not here. Come to the house with me."

"No!" she exploded, then took a deep breath and started again. "I'm busy. If you want to talk to me it will have to be here."

He sighed. "All right, but let's go upstairs. Peg can handle things down here."

He didn't give her a chance to protest, but took her by the arm and led her out of the shop and upstairs to her apartment.

This wasn't going at all well. She hated him for what he'd done to her but still his touch could turn her bones to water. She didn't want to be alone with him but she knew they had to talk sometime and she couldn't refuse without seeming childish.

By all means let's not be childish, she chided herself. *You were a child when he walked out on you the first time. At least have a little pride and act like an adult now.*

She unlocked the door and led the way into the living room. It was chilly in the apartment and she turned up the thermostat but didn't take off her sweater or ask Peter to remove his jacket. She didn't want him to think she was settling in for a long session. It was imperative to her sanity that they get this over quickly.

Peter stood by the picture window looking out at the churning waters of the bay and he didn't look at her as he said, "I've withdrawn my objections to the dissolution of our marriage. You won't have any further trouble about it."

Gina put her hand across her midsection as she lowered herself to sit on the couch and it took her a minute to catch her breath and realize that he hadn't punched her in the stomach with his fist, only his words.

She knew she should say something but couldn't trust herself to speak. What was the matter with her anyway? This was what she'd wanted, wasn't it? Now she could be free to either continue as she had been or find another man to love.

The idea was so ludicrous that it made her giggle with suppressed hysteria and it was then that Peter turned to look down at her. "What's so funny?" he demanded.

"N-nothing. I'm sorry," she answered in a voice tight with pain.

Funny? Oh no, it wasn't funny. How could a lifetime of quiet desperation be funny? Peter's revenge was even more complete than he realized. He'd left her with a future so lonely and bleak that she didn't dare contemplate it. Before he came back into her life she'd had Stewart. She could have loved Stewart in a quiet mature way and been reasonably happy with him, but now all hope of a husband and family were denied her. How could she give herself to another man when she was a part of Peter and he was a part of her?

Peter was again looking out at the bay as he resumed the conversation. "The house is yours as I told you it would be. I hope you will live in it but if not it would be best to either sell or rent it. It mustn't be left unoccupied, and maintaining a caretaker is expensive."

He shifted restlessly and clutched the sheer curtain in his fist. "I've also made arrangements for you to receive alimony. You'll be sent a check at the first of every month. If you feel you need more just contact my attorney and he'll arrange it."

Gina sat hunched over, numb with misery. She didn't even try to protest. Peter would never believe that she didn't want his money. All she could do was return the checks each month unopened until he finally understood that she would never accept them.

As for the house . . . she couldn't think about that now.

Gradually Gina realized that Peter had stopped speaking and an uneasy silence had grown between them. It was her turn to say something, but what. *Thank you Peter for being so generous, that's a lot of money for a one-night stand?* Or maybe, *Don't leave me, Peter, I can't live without you?* If she begged, would he keep her around for those few times when he had no one else to warm his bed?

She clenched her jaws to stifle a sob. She had to stop this. She was on the verge of fragmenting into little pieces that could never be put back together again.

Peter turned slowly and their eyes met. He looked awful and she wondered if he'd been drinking and was going to be sick, but she knew he hadn't been. He was cold sober, but something was bothering him.

Maybe it was his conscience. Did he realize what he was putting her through and find it distasteful? Did he understand that he should have left her untouched if he planned to throw her away? Was he finding vengeance bitter and unfulfilling?

"Don't you have anything to say to me?" he asked softly. He sounded so forlorn, as though he really wanted her to talk to him.

She shook her head, only wanting to get this over with. If he didn't leave soon she was going to come unglued right in front of him.

He started to walk toward her but then stopped and

turned toward the door instead. "Good-bye, Gina," he muttered hoarsely and began moving down the short hall.

"Peter." Gina was as surprised as he to hear herself call his name, but when he stopped and turned to look at her she knew what she had to say.

"What did I do wrong?" It came out as little more than a whisper.

He stared at her. "What did *you* do wrong?" he asked as though he didn't understand the question.

She nodded. "When—when we made love." Her voice was a little stronger now, but still reedy. "What did I do wrong? Why were you so disappointed?"

Peter still stared at her, seemingly unable to comprehend what she was saying. He walked slowly back to the couch and sat down beside her. Gently he took her face in his hands and tipped it so he could devour her with his eyes. "Oh dear Lord," he breathed, "is that what you thought? That I was disappointed?"

The tip of her tongue flicked between her dry lips as her gaze roamed over his white, taut features. "Yes." She was back to a whisper again. "I wanted so to please you but I didn't know how."

Peter's face seemed to crumble and with a low groan he pulled her into his arms and buried his head in her sweater-clad shoulder. Gina held him and stroked her fingers through his wind-tousled hair, instinctively understanding the massive effort he was making to regain the self-control that had so mysteriously abandoned him. He held her in a crushing embrace but she made no protest as she sought to relieve in some small way his obvious torment. What had she said that upset him so?

They sat wrapped in each other's arms for several minutes, not speaking until gradually Peter's heaving shoulders quieted and his hold on her lessened to a more comfortable degree. Finally he straightened and pressed her head against his jacket-covered chest. She had the impression that he didn't want her to look at him just yet and she relaxed against him and put her arms around his waist.

His heart beat erratically beneath her ear and she knew she wanted nothing more from life than to spend it in the arms of this complex man who baffled her at every turn. If his conditions for that were impossible so was the thought of living without him.

After a while, Peter's breathing and heartbeat returned to normal and it was only then that he spoke. His voice was still shaky as he rubbed his cheek in her ebony hair and said, "I love you, Gina. I love you so much that I honestly don't think I can survive if I lose you again."

Gina caught her breath and held it as she looked up at him and gasped, "But you said . . ."

He looked down at her and she saw that his eyes were red-rimmed and his face looked ravaged. "I know what I said. I said that you had killed the love I once felt for you, but even as I said it I knew I was lying. In my arrogance I chose to believe the evidence of the picture and Mel Calicutt, and the past seven years without you have been hell. If I'd known where you were I would have come for you but, God forgive me, I believed my parents and Veronica when they said you had left San Francisco with Calicutt so I didn't search for you. I did write to you in care of your parents, though. Please believe that."

Gina was trembling with shock and relief. Peter loved her! She didn't know which was greater, the shock of his confession or the relief that he returned her love.

"I know," she said as she unzipped his windbreaker and pushed it aside so she could eliminate a layer of the heavy clothing that restricted their contact. "I talked to Mama. She admitted that the letters had come to the house and she burned them."

She laid her head against the soft beige velour of his shirt and he began to unbutton the buttons on her heavy sweater. "I can't really blame her," he said as the first button came undone and he moved on to the second. "She had good reason to hate me and want to keep us apart."

The second button opened and he moved to the third. "When you didn't answer my letters I told myself I was a fool for wanting you and tried to erase you from my mind."

He sighed as the third button was released and the sweater parted to allow his hand to stroke her breast through the cotton material of her orchid blouse. "It was impossible. No matter how hard I worked or how far I traveled you were always there to haunt me."

Gina slipped her hands under his loose shirt and lightly massaged the sparse flesh of his bare back. He was so thin, almost bony, and she wondered if he'd been eating enough.

He stretched and almost purred as he said, "Oh, that feels so good. I can't get enough of your touch."

"Can't you?" she asked as she continued the movement. "Then what did I do wrong the other night? Why did you leave me so abruptly?"

He moaned and held her closer as though using her as a shield against the pain her question seemed to cause him. "You didn't do anything wrong, sweetheart. I left because I thought you wanted me to."

Again she raised her head to look at him. "Wanted

you to?" she asked in amazement. "Why did you think that?"

"Because of the way I'd treated you!" The words seemed to be torn from him. "Gina, don't you honestly understand? I had just forced myself on you—"

"No!" Gina protested but he touched his fingers to her lips to stop her.

"Yes, I did. I deliberately seduced you against your will because I was desperate. You refused to consider living with me, being my wife, and I was sure that if we just once made love you would know how I felt about you and realize that you felt the same way."

Gina kissed his fingers then moved her head to dislodge them. "But why didn't you just tell me—?"

"I couldn't." He pushed her head back against his chest and stroked her short hair. "I had to protect myself. I couldn't have stood it if you'd told me you didn't want my love."

His arms tightened around her. "Darling, I don't think you understand just how shattered I was by that picture and Mel's confession. Whether or not you were a virgin wouldn't have mattered to me if you hadn't used it as an excuse not to go to bed with me until we were married. I wanted you so bad I would have done anything, but I loved you too and wanted you for a wife. I was so proud and happy on our wedding day and then that picture was delivered. I thought I'd been played for a fool, that you only wanted my money after all, and I couldn't handle it."

She tried to say something but again he stopped her with a finger to her lips. "No, let me finish. I ran away. It was a cowardly thing to do, but I had to be alone to try to sort out my hurt and rage and come to terms with it. For two months I was lost. Literally. I just got in my car and drove. Most of that time is a blur, but when I finally came out of it I realized that I still wanted you, needed you, loved you. I went back to San Francisco to get you and try to make a go of the marriage that had started out so disastrously but you were gone. You know the rest."

Gina had been so engrossed in his explanation that she hadn't noticed when he unbuttoned her blouse and released the front catch on her bra. But now as his firm hand cupped the nude mound of her full breast a wave of heat swept through her and she reached up and pulled his head down so that his mouth teased her erect nipple.

He lifted her and laid her across his lap where his lips and tongue had easier access to her creamy fragrant flesh. She clung to him and nibbled lightly on his neck, causing him to shiver with pleasure as his hand on her leg moved slowly upward. He raised his head and looked at her, his eyes misty with desire.

"How could you possibly have thought I was disappointed in our love-making?" he murmured thickly. "It was all I had ever hoped it would be and more, except . . ."

The joy she had felt at his words was tempered. "Except what?" she whispered anxiously.

"Except that never once in those seven years had it occurred to me that you might be telling the truth, that you were still a virgin. When I realized how—innocent—you were I—"

He lifted her away from him almost roughly and sat up, raking his hands through his light hair in a gesture of agitation. "Gina, if I'd been any kind of man I'd have withdrawn and left you alone. It was inexcusable of me to continue, but I couldn't have stopped if my life had depended on it. I'd waited too long and we'd gone too far. I had to complete it!"

Gina felt giddy with happiness. He was upset with himself, not with her! She sat up beside him and took his hand in hers. "Of course you had to complete it, darling. I'd have killed you if you hadn't! Is that all that was bothering you?"

He lifted their twined hands and kissed the back of hers. "No, that's not all," he said wearily. "In that blinding moment of truth I knew that I had wronged you unforgivably and wasted seven long years of our lives in a torment of my own making instead of spending them happily together, loving each other and raising a family."

Gina knew it would take him a long time to exorcise his guilt, but she also knew she must not let it weigh too heavily on his conscience. She removed her hand from his and put it on his thigh, then began caressing him with her fingers. "It's not too late to start that family," she said softly.

The muscles beneath her hand twitched and his voice was husky as he said, "If you keep that up the first one is going to be conceived right here on the rug."

For a moment she continued the sensuous massage, then shyly she began to remove her unfastened sweater, blouse and bra and dropped to her knees on the thickly padded carpet. She lifted her arms to Peter in mute invitation and the naked hunger in his eyes was the acceptance she'd longed for.

With an unconscious gracefulness he pulled his shirt over his head and knelt in front of her. She put her hands on his bare shoulders and gently kneaded the firm flesh and muscle.

He moaned deep in his throat and took her in his

arms. "I love you, Gina," he murmured, and there was something akin to reverence in his tone. "I've loved you from the first day we met and I'll love you until the day I die. Don't ever doubt that."

Her happiness was so great that she was sure it was shining from her violet eyes as she put her arms around his neck and lifted her face to his. "I've never belonged to any man but you, Peter," she told him softly. "In all those years without you I wasn't even tempted, that's why I couldn't marry Stewart. I'm a one-man woman, darling, and you're the man."

His head lowered and his eager mouth found hers and sent liquid fire racing through her veins. She pressed herself against him and gloried in his masculinity. As he shifted her carefully to a reclining position she knew that she would never again have to deny the passion that blazed between them. A passion so wild that she doubted it could ever be tamed. She sincerely hoped that it couldn't.

IT'S YOUR OWN SPECIAL TIME

Contemporary romances for today's women.
Each month, six very special love stories will be yours
from SILHOUETTE.

$1.75 each

☐ 100 Stanford	☐ 127 Roberts	☐ 155 Hampson	☐ 182 Clay
☐ 101 Hardy	☐ 128 Hampson	☐ 156 Sawyer	☐ 183 Stanley
☐ 102 Hastings	☐ 129 Converse	☐ 157 Vitek	☐ 184 Hardy
☐ 103 Cork	☐ 130 Hardy	☐ 158 Reynolds	☐ 185 Hampson
☐ 104 Vitek	☐ 131 Stanford	☐ 159 Tracy	☐ 186 Howard
☐ 105 Eden	☐ 132 Wisdom	☐ 160 Hampson	☐ 187 Scott
☐ 106 Dailey	☐ 133 Rowe	☐ 161 Trent	☐ 188 Cork
☐ 107 Bright	☐ 134 Charles	☐ 162 Ashby	☐ 189 Stephens
☐ 108 Hampson	☐ 135 Logan	☐ 163 Roberts	☐ 190 Hampson
☐ 109 Vernon	☐ 136 Hampson	☐ 164 Browning	☐ 191 Browning
☐ 110 Trent	☐ 137 Hunter	☐ 165 Young	☐ 192 John
☐ 111 South	☐ 138 Wilson	☐ 166 Wisdom	☐ 193 Trent
☐ 112 Stanford	☐ 139 Vitek	☐ 167 Hunter	☐ 194 Barry
☐ 113 Browning	☐ 140 Erskine	☐ 168 Carr	☐ 195 Dailey
☐ 114 Michaels	☐ 142 Browning	☐ 169 Scott	☐ 196 Hampson
☐ 115 John	☐ 143 Roberts	☐ 170 Ripy	☐ 197 Summers
☐ 116 Lindley	☐ 144 Goforth	☐ 171 Hill	☐ 198 Hunter
☐ 117 Scott	☐ 145 Hope	☐ 172 Browning	☐ 199 Roberts
☐ 118 Dailey	☐ 146 Michaels	☐ 173 Camp	☐ 200 Lloyd
☐ 119 Hampson	☐ 147 Hampson	☐ 174 Sinclair	☐ 201 Starr
☐ 120 Carroll	☐ 148 Cork	☐ 175 Jarrett	☐ 202 Hampson
☐ 121 Langan	☐ 149 Saunders	☐ 176 Vitek	☐ 203 Browning
☐ 122 Scofield	☐ 150 Major	☐ 177 Dailey	☐ 204 Carroll
☐ 123 Sinclair	☐ 151 Hampson	☐ 178 Hampson	☐ 205 Maxam
☐ 124 Beckman	☐ 152 Halston	☐ 179 Beckman	☐ 206 Manning
☐ 125 Bright	☐ 153 Dailey	☐ 180 Roberts	☐ 207 Windham
☐ 126 St. George	☐ 154 Beckman	☐ 181 Terrill	

IT'S YOUR OWN SPECIAL TIME
Contemporary romances for today's women.
Each month, six very special love stories will be yours
from SILHOUETTE. Look for them wherever books are sold
or order now from the coupon below.

$1.95 each

☐ 208 Halston	☐ 228 King	☐ 248 St. George	☐ 268 Hunter
☐ 209 LaDame	☐ 229 Thornton	☐ 249 Scofield	☐ 269 Smith
☐ 210 Eden	☐ 230 Stevens	☐ 250 Hampson	☐ 270 Camp
☐ 211 Walters	☐ 231 Dailey	☐ 251 Wilson	☐ 271 Allison
☐ 212 Young	☐ 232 Hampson	☐ 252 Roberts	☐ 272 Forrest
☐ 213 Dailey	☐ 233 Vernon	☐ 253 James	☐ 273 Beckman
☐ 214 Hampson	☐ 234 Smith	☐ 254 Palmer	☐ 274 Roberts
☐ 215 Roberts	☐ 235 James	☐ 255 Smith	☐ 275 Browning
☐ 216 Saunders	☐ 236 Maxam	☐ 256 Hampson	☐ 276 Vernon
☐ 217 Vitek	☐ 237 Wilson	☐ 257 Hunter	☐ 277 Wilson
☐ 218 Hunter	☐ 238 Cork	☐ 258 Ashby	☐ 278 Hunter
☐ 219 Cork	☐ 239 McKay	☐ 259 English	☐ 279 Ashby
☐ 220 Hampson	☐ 240 Hunter	☐ 260 Martin	☐ 280 Roberts
☐ 221 Browning	☐ 241 Wisdom	☐ 261 Saunders	☐ 281 Lovan
☐ 222 Carroll	☐ 242 Brooke	☐ 262 John	☐ 282 Halldorson
☐ 223 Summers	☐ 243 Saunders	☐ 263 Wilson	☐ 283 Payne
☐ 224 Langan	☐ 244 Sinclair	☐ 264 Vine	☐ 284 Young
☐ 225 St. George	☐ 245 Trent	☐ 265 Adams	☐ 285 Gray
☐ 226 Hamson	☐ 246 Carroll	☐ 266 Trent	
☐ 227 Beckman	☐ 247 Halldorson	☐ 267 Chase	

SILHOUETTE BOOKS, Department SB/1
1230 Avenue of the Americas
New York, NY 10020

Please send me the books I have checked above. I am enclosing $_____
(please add 75¢ to cover postage and handling. NYS and NYC residents please
add appropriate sales tax). Send check or money order—no cash or C.O.D.'s
please. Allow six weeks for delivery.

NAME _____

ADDRESS _____

CITY _____ STATE/ZIP _____

Let Silhouette Inspirations show you a world of Christian love and romance...
for 15 days, free.

If you want to read wholesome love stories...with characters whose spiritual values are as meaningful as yours...then you'll want to read Silhouette Inspirations™ novels. You'll experience all of love's conflicts and pleasures—and the joy of happy endings—with people who share your beliefs and goals.

These books are written by Christian authors...Arlene James, Patti Beckman, Debbie Macomber, and more...for Christian readers. Each 192-page volume gives you tender romance with a message of hope and faith...and of course, a happy ending.

We think you'll be so delighted with Silhouette Inspirations, you won't want to miss a single one! We'd like to send you 2 books each month, as soon as they are published, through our Home Subscription Service. Look them over for 15 days, free. If you enjoy them as much as we think you will, pay the enclosed invoice. If not, simply return them and owe nothing.

A world of Christian love and spirituality is waiting for you...in the pages of Silhouette Inspirations novels. Return the coupon today!